In The Mind of a Young Entrepreneur

—ɷ—

Michael Gentile & Allon Avgi

ISBN: 1503093379
ISBN 13: 9781503093379
Library of Congress Control Number: 2014919812
CreateSpace Independent Publishing Platform
North Charleston, South Carolina

1

As a young boy, I always knew I would be rich. I always relished in the thought of seizing every dream I ever had, of living a life chosen for play. I always envisioned the day when I could frolic freely throughout the world without the pressure of money, with the liberty to pursue rather than maintain. I always imagined how it must feel to adorn yourself with distinctive badges of your worth, accomplishment, and triumph; to explode into every room you walk into. This fascination wasn't a want or a hope or an aspiration. I needed to be rich. To fall short would mean a long, agonizing fall to the bottom, cursed by what could have been.

Dollar bills circulated through my young, famished mind like debris in a tornado. I sat in the middle, a mere spectator to the cyclone of desire in which I was trapped hopefully, not hopelessly. The thick, smooth, viscous texture of the bills caused my fingers to stick. The bills melded to my hand, belongingly, offering comfort to both myself and the very spirits living within the prizes. I felt everyone else who had once held the bill, every register it had called home, every vending machine through which it had stubbornly slid. They all told a story. And I sat on the edge of my seat for each and every one.

The smell often beckoned to my nostrils, tempting and inciting my mind to travel to all new places of longing. The color assaulted my eyes with its most subtle appearances, teaching me through shock to never look past the light and dark greens that have made our country what it is today. George Washington's stern, potent face taught me long ago that a dollar wasn't a bag of chips or a pack of cards; it was an opportunity. It all made so much sense to me. The little digits and numbers. The vines and leaves. The pyramid and seal. In God we trust. Each clue opened up a new layer within my own being, another level deeper down through which I could find myself.

Today, I stand hollow. I have more money than I could ever dream of, but the costs of accumulating it all have ravaged the foundation beneath. I am a towering, extravagant mansion of great awe to all who pass, but of great shock and despair to all who actually enter through my doors. I am no home. I offer no comfort or love or ease.

Everything around me serves as a gaudy, debilitating reminder of regret. Instead of offering me the freedom and pleasure that I had once dreamed they would, all my possessions do is add weight to my already buckling shoulders, forcing me to collapse. All the cars, the properties, the women, and even all the little dollar bills mean nothing now. I don't deserve two nickels to rub together.

Only eighteen years old, I have much time. Much torment awaits me in my retirement. The world is at my fingertips, but I merely sit with closed fists, holding on to the money that cuts deeper into my soul with every passing minute. All it is now is something to hold. I have already paid my greatest cost.

2

It did not take long for me to stop dreaming about money and start taking action to accumulate it. I was never a kid of "I want" or "Give me this." I quickly adopted the mindset of "See that; watch me take it." And that's exactly what I did. By the age of five, I had already mastered the greatest secret of making money. I was a ruthless child in a world of passive adults.

I was only in kindergarten when I first began to thumb around the business world. I took full advantage of the immortality provided by being cute, small, and silly. Little did most people know, I wasn't any of the three. I was not cute, but tenacious; not small, but unsuspected; and not silly, but deceptive. I will always remember the first time I used all those qualities to pull the wool over the eyes of my peers.

I've never been a man, or boy, of expense. The goal was always to obtain, rather than buy. All items had to be recycled in the chain of sale eventually, so why lose to gain something that eventually must be lost? Bottom line, if it was free, it was for me. And if it was free for me, there would always be a profit down the road. It didn't matter what the item was. My first ever plan circulated around a delightful bouquet of flowers.

My mother had quite the garden when I was a little boy. The colors splashed life all throughout the property, transforming a once typical house into a natural and complex spectacle. She slaved over it for hours each day. It seemed to be the one thing that she could do without thinking, without actually having to try. And it showed. The best parts of my mother stayed with her garden. The worst parts rested with me.

One morning, I decided to pick my mother's flowers and sell them to my classmates for a dollar each. All little kids carry a dollar with them. I was sure that some of them wouldn't hesitate to substitute their daily ice-cream bar for a pretty, smelly tulip.

On the first day, I only swiped about a dozen flowers. And I made twelve dollars. It was an unbelievable amount of money for me at the time. Twelve breathtaking cloth portraits of George Washington. Twelve autographs from the Treasurer of the United States and the Secretary of the Treasury. I was on top of the world for the first time, and there was no going down from there.

I stepped up production more and more the next two days, leaving my mother's beloved garden barren. Consequence didn't resonate with me at the time. The only consequence I knew was money, and that was not a fate I shied away from. It didn't take long for my sales to break through the kindergarten ceiling and make their way around the entire elementary school. I was the guy with the goods.

It also didn't take long before the cafeteria realized a startling drop-off in snack sales and murmurs began to circulate. I was notorious, the most notorious five-year-old florist of my generation. *The Man* was ringing for me. Fifty-eight dollars in, it was time to face the music. I lawyered up and made my way to the court-house, right in between the nurse's office and the custodian closet.

The principal was a sweet middle-aged woman by the name of Ms. White. She wasn't the most jubilant of souls, but it was easy to tell that she truly cared for each and every kid that walked through her doors. A tall woman, she had old, pale skin and a very firm, strong haircut. Her straight hair did not droop past her ears but instead coagulated above her actual head, taking the form of a large beehive. She dressed very professionally—no dresses or frilly shirts. She was a leader. She was never mean. However, it still took people by surprise whenever she made a joke.

I walked into the main office on that Thursday morning, profits in backpack, and sat down at the request of the secretary. I waited for about three minutes on the green-cushioned, wooden chair before getting called. I walked in confidently, as if I had no clue why I was in the principal's office in the first place. When I sat down, she stood up and slowly walked around her desk to talk to me more closely. She leaned on her desk, never breaking eye contact.

"So, I've heard quite a few things about you the past couple days," she said. She expected me to respond, but I honestly had no idea what to say. I was still in my playing dumb phase.

"I've heard that you've been selling flowers. Is that true?" This being our first encounter, she didn't know what type of kid she was dealing with. She may have been taking my silence for weakness and didn't want to upset me by pushing too hard.

I nodded, still not saying a word.

"That's very nice of you, but you aren't really supposed to do that. You can't take money from your classmates." She paused briefly, perhaps waiting for me to answer. "Do you understand that?" She was speaking very slowly.

"Yeah," I said. "I'm sorry. I didn't know."

"Do you have the money with you now?"

I nodded and took my backpack off. I unzipped the top compartment and pulled out a crumpled wad of singles. I didn't hand it to her though.

"I'm sorry, Ms. White, but I can't give you this money," I said.

"Why is that?" she asked.

"Well, I didn't want to tell anyone this, but I need it for my mommy." There was no going back now. The first lie was in the open, and my only hope was to lie my way out from there.

"What do you mean?" She tilted her head.

"Well, my mom is sick right now. And I heard my mom and dad talking about how much money it costs to make her all better, so I wanted to help. I sold her flowers to get enough money to make her all better. I'm sorry, but I can't give it to you."

Through Ms. White's eyes, I saw her heart break. It was as if all her previous convictions had melted right off her face. A once rough and rigid countenance, her face immediately slackened, leaving all her facial skin smooth and loose. Her bottom lip stuck out and her head stood up in surprise. She had never heard such a heart-warming sentiment in all her years of supervising tiny booger-faced kids. I tried to keep my emotions steady.

Ms. White never even responded. She proceeded to walk around to the other side of her desk, reach down into her pocketbook, and pull out her light brown, leather wallet. She walked back around toward me and gave me a fifty-dollar bill followed by a long, sappy, awkward hug.

"If you ever need anything," she said, "don't hesitate to come by and ask." She then gestured me to leave her office, still gleaming with emotion. She was so touched by what I had said. I had made a serious impact on her, and it was all a lie. I didn't know whether to be proud or ashamed. I took my fifty dollars, wrapped it around the rest of the money, and quickly stuffed it into my backpack. I smiled at Ms. White and scurried out of the office like I stole something.

When I got home that evening, I spoke as little as possible to my parents. I ate dinner and went straight to my room. I took all the money out of my backpack and put it into my piggy bank. I went to sleep, thinking that I had made it out alive, ready to call it quits on my florist career.

The next day, I walked into the school to the sight of banners, tables, and heaps of flowers in front of the main office. The overhanging banner read, "Flowers for the Fight." Two adults sat at the table. They greeted me and smiled. There were kids and teachers and janitors and all types of people waiting in line to pay for flowers, and thus to donate to my sick mother's fight against illness.

The next thing I saw was Ms. White in the middle of a conversation with other teachers, waving at me from down the hallway. She ended her conversation and began to approach me with a smile on her face.

"Isn't this great?" she exclaimed. "Your mom is going to be better in no time. And it's all thanks to you. She is going to be so proud."

I nodded grudgingly and allowed her to go on her way. I knew I was fucked now. It was a miracle that my mother hadn't noticed all her flowers were missing. Now, it was too dire a case to even salvage. That was one of the longest school days of my life. Sitting in class, fielding a billion and one questions, lying to everybody I knew, and ultimately waiting for my execution.

On my way to the bus at the end of the day, Ms. White approached me. Kneeling down, she handed me a fat envelope, gave me a big smile, and patted me on the back. Still walking, I opened the envelope. It was filled with cash. Ones, fives, tens, twenties. The shock knocked me off my stride, jolting my mind into a whole new dimension. I knew I was in deep shit now. However, I couldn't help but smile every time I glimpsed into that envelope.

When I arrived at home, I tried to sneak into the house without being detected. I was cautious and measured with every step. Luckily, my mom wasn't there to take me off the bus. I didn't see her downstairs, either. I climbed up the stairs, thinking myself to be in the clear. I sprinted into my room, closed the door with a sigh of relief, and sat down triumphantly. Behind me, I heard the footsteps of a pissed-off woman.

Apparently, someone had called my house to give their best wishes to my sick mother and ended up telling her what I had been up to for the past week. My mother was absolutely livid. She stood before me with a smug stare of condemnation. She had all my money in her right hand and her eyes on my every heartbeat.

She drove me back to the school, forced me to confess to Ms. White, and gave all the money back. Needless to say, I was forbidden from recess for the rest of the school year and from freedom for the rest of my childhood. I was only five, and I had already been snitched on, prosecuted, sentenced, and forced to pay reparations.

In the following months, I didn't sulk in my failure and punishment. I identified my mistakes and thought how I would fix them if given another opportunity. I had gotten my first whiff of money, six hundred and seventy-two green, little beauties. The sensation of wealth had entered my mind and was now trapped. I would not be denied. I would be reunited with my loves before long.

I had already met the dead end at the close of the tunnel. There was no longer anything to be afraid of, besides not finding what lay on the other side.

3

In the aftermath of my florist business, I didn't take much time off. I started experimenting with new projects. Learning from my first experience, I knew I had to approach my plans a little bit differently. I was already under watch as it was.

I figured I would start off clean. I didn't want to push my luck and floor the gas pedal too early. But I would soon learn that everything is infinitely harder when you follow all the rules. There are some standards that you have to squeeze through or slide around just to avoid the extra fuss. Whether it is a paper route or investment banking, the temptation is there for any businessman. Over time, that pressure tends to wear you down, eventually causing your morals to bend or even cave.

For the next seven years, I was a relentless rugrat entrepreneur, turning nothing into something everywhere I went. My feverish passion for money burned deep well before I ever laid a finger on a dollar. After holding six hundred and seventy-two of them in my tiny, delicate hands, it simply became an obsession. As messed up as it may sound, those everyday greenbacks were like heroin to me. Always chasing that first high, I sought more and more until the item finally consumed me. However, working for money didn't feel like an addiction. It was what I had become.

At the age of six, I opened a lemonade stand. I know, it was terribly boring and clichéd, but hey, I had just gotten out on parole. My P.O. had her eyes on me at all times, and I wasn't trying to cause any ripples. I was on "smile and wave" mode, being a basic little kid in a basic little world. Profit dripped in like a broken, leaky faucet. Every droplet fell slower than the previous one. I felt like I was dying of dehydration in the desert, my muscles and organs shriveling within me, losing consciousness of my impending doom, imagining things that were never to come. But instead, I was at a beverage stand twenty feet from the front door of my house.

I couldn't endure the suffering of running a politically correct lemonade stand. After a while, the lemons started to irritate my hands and eyes. It was not even good lemonade. Fed up, I left my post for a few minutes, walked down to the local grocery store with all the money I had made, and bought three giant jugs of lemonade. I still had profit to spare and more lemonade than anybody could ever want to squeeze. And the lemonade actually tasted good. For generations, kids had been running lemonade stands the wrong way.

There wasn't even anything wrong with what I did. I merely invested my income to bring in more income. It was more efficient, much easier, branching off the main river, a shortcut. I could have just worked harder and squeezed more lemons, but what would that have done in the long run? There is always a better way, a different way.

I followed that procedure every day for an entire summer, gathered a following of regular shoppers, and eventually called it quits once the school year swung around again. I had to find a new project, one that could endure the test of time.

Always a decent student who didn't mind work, I had a name for myself in school. My classmates trusted my ability to get all my second-grade work done. You know, addition and subtraction, shapes and colors, spelling and punctuation, tough stuff. Well, after a few weeks in class, I began selling my services. And boy was the demand high.

I began doing homework for all my classmates, and when I say "all," I mean all. Every day after school, I would go to the library, do my own work, and then make twenty-one copies of it. The librarian never even charged me for the copies. She rejoiced in the fact that a seven-year-old wanted to spend his time surrounded by mountains of old dusty books. From there, I would ride my bike to each and every one of my classmates' houses and drop off my answers. They would copy them in their own handwriting and hand them in the next morning.

It was actually quite a brilliant operation. The work could never be traced back to me, since everybody had the same answers in different handwritings. I would get paid in whatever I wanted. I obviously preferred money, but I didn't hesitate to accept snacks or toys or even kisses from some of the girls. It wasn't any extra work for me. All I had to do was press *copy*. By the end of the school year, my entire bicycle route was down to twenty minutes.

It only fell through when the class idiot forgot to copy the homework in his own handwriting and decided to hand in the copy I gave him. The teacher, relieved to have finally caught the slip, ended it all right there. It was a good run. My bad boy reputation was actively spreading, even catching the eyes of some of the older kids.

I began associating more and more with older children, both as a protégé and a bitch. It didn't matter to me though. There is nothing cooler to a little kid than hanging out with older kids. You idolize them. You would do anything for them. Trust me.

I basically ran missions for all my older friends. I retrieved things, did chores, even got girls' phone numbers for them. They paid me with money quite often, but even more so with respect. I learned much from all of them and grew very quickly as a result, too quickly. It didn't take long before I had broken out of my immature trance and moved on. They were all perching on one level as I was jumping and clawing my way up for more and more.

Tired of my laboring and dragging incomes, I resorted back to my old tactics, the ones that put my career on lockdown for quite some time. I was a liar again. After all, why not? I was still a kid, still only nine years old. I had already made it through four years of doing unethical shit and nothing bad had happened to me. I had to use my cuteness while I still had it.

One day, I had the idea to put on proper clothes and walk to the local bakery around closing time. I pleaded with the owner to allow me to take all the leftover food to the church where it could be donated to the less fortunate. After melting his heart and retrieving all the food, I made my way to the local grocery store and sold all the baked goods at the door. I even enlisted the help of some of my friends in order to make us look official. I paid them all a dollar per day. It wasn't even stealing. I was just selling people literal garbage, and they ate it up big-time.

My most ruthless business venture came when I was ten years old. I had recently gotten into a huge fight with my parents. They weren't too happy with all my shady activities and condemned me to stay at home for the next month. This was sure to kill my business and send me into a month-long withdrawal period. Well, so they thought.

One day when both my parents had gone to work, I was left home alone without a babysitter. I woke up very early and formulated a devious plan, a deviously brilliant plan. I scurried around, set everything up, and called some friends to help me. By 8:30 a.m., I had orchestrated an all-out garage sale. My entire living room was now on my front lawn: vases, picture frames, tribal decorations, curtains, knickknacks, antiques, ottomans, little glass ornaments. All of which were now being shipped off the property by the boatload, never to return again.

As you could imagine, I made a lot of money and got in a lot of trouble. Luckily, I had hidden the money, twelve hundred dollars in cold hard cash, underneath the deck in my backyard. Unluckily, my parents ended up doing the same thing I had, but with my bedroom.

Before long, I was sleeping in an empty, white-walled room on a bare mattress.

When I was eleven, I basically opened a portable supply shop. I bought school supplies in bulk, using my mother's coupons, and carried them with me around school. However, the customer base was weak in the beginning, and I took it upon myself to increase demand. Whether my classmates liked it or not, they needed school supplies. They just didn't know it yet.

I began ripping up folders, crumpling up notebooks, and snapping pencils whenever the opportunity presented itself. I would run in at recess while everyone was out playing and destroy everything systematically, just enough to force sales but not enough to cause a stir. I then swooped in with new and improved supplies. It was like selling candy to a baby, a baby who had just gotten her lollipop ripped out of her mouth and smashed on the floor.

There were many accusations against me by the end of the year, but nothing I couldn't evade. My business eventually slowed, fizzling out before any real cash was summoned. And with that final business venture, elementary school was over. I was now twelve years old. All those years of being focused upon under a microscope were over. I was a liberated man, free to start anew. This was the time to strike.

In middle school, I discovered a wonderful phenomenon called peer pressure. Modern society had already done all my work for me. My new student body was putty in the hands of whatever was cool at the time.

They were all puppets. Once the curtains opened, there was no stopping what I could do.

I began selling cigarettes. I would steal them from wherever I could get them, whether it was my father, my teachers, my older friends, or even stores. I became more notorious than I had ever been, but only among my clientele. This time, no adults had knowledge of my work. Teachers had almost grown accustomed to seeing their students puffing away on cigarettes and no longer worried about how they were getting them. I was a shadow, within it all, but without a trace.

Finally, I had something I could maintain and develop. Cash rolled in regularly, and I adopted a firm approach that couldn't be beaten. I rose to social prominence throughout the district without ever playing one ball game, swimming at one beach, or hosting one party. All I did for seven years was make money. Nine thousand one hundred and twenty-eight dollars later, there was not a ceiling in sight. I was the best, and everyone knew it.

4

One Tuesday a couple weeks after my thirteenth birthday, I came home to a beautiful Mercedes parked in my driveway. It was one of those jaw-dropping, heart-stopping beauties that you see on the covers of rich people magazines. It was dignified, yet edgy and cool. With a metallic silver paint job, the car was built for speed, judging by its height and aerodynamic accessories, but also for luxury, assuming from the convertible top and regal grill. Every inch of the car screamed wealth.

I walked through the gate leading to the backyard, dropped off the day's earnings in the usual spot, and entered the house through the back screen door. Usually, I would just go up to my room, evading every question I could. But this time, I stuck around, looking for the mystery man with the magic keys. As soon as I cleared the kitchen and poked my head into the dining room, I saw him.

He was sitting at one end of the dinner table, opposite from my mother and father. He wore a stylish gray sports jacket over a black cotton dress shirt, a stunning silver watch, and a pair of shiny black dress shoes. His hair was greased back, but not in a cheap gaudy way. He wore his haircut very confidently, as if it was calibrated precisely to suit him and his intentions. He was clean-shaven with a strong jawline and smooth facial skin. He oozed professionalism and class. And he couldn't have been older than thirty-five. He was younger than my parents.

It took a few moments before the man realized I was wading in the shadows of the dining room. But once he saw me, he immediately dropped what was he doing, walked over, and shook my hand with a lethal smile on his face.

"Arthur Swezey," he said. "But you can call me Swezey." He introduced himself like a classic businessman, keeping his cool and ensuring that I would remember his name.

Reacting to my silence, my father intervened and responded for me. "This is my son, Phineas." Now to me: "Arthur is a friend of ours. He is going to help us make a little extra money."

As soon as I heard the word *money*, I snapped out of my paralysis and jumped into the conversation. "Money, huh?" I asked. "What do you do?"

Mr. Swezey then gave me a half smirk, half grin that split my entire universe into two equally unfamiliar fragments. It was a countenance of curiosity and surprise, but also of conviction and experience. It was as if nothing could shock him, but I came close. He buckled a bit but did not go down. I hadn't even heard him say more than six words and he was already the coolest guy I had ever met.

"What do I do?" Mr. Swezey restated. "Well, kid, I make money."

"What do you mean?" I asked.

He looked at my parents, smiling, wondering what he was supposed to tell me. My parents returned the gaze, also curious about how he was going to respond. Playing it off, Mr. Swezey asked, "Why do you ask?"

"Well, I consider myself quite the businessman."

"Okay, what do you do?" He asked.

"What do I do?" I restated, just as Mr. Swezey had before. Glancing at my parents, their eyes could have very well been staring at me from the gates of hell. "It's not important. Don't worry about it."

"Exactly," he said. "It's not always important how you make money. It's just a yes or no question. Do you make money?"

Having my entire personal religion set on this concept, this question took a significant amount of philosophical thought to answer. No matter how much money I thought I had made, it would never compare to Mr. Rico Suave standing in front of me. And it's not like I had a real job in which I actually worked for the money. Almost every cent I had ever made came from a hustle, a scam, a trick that took advantage of stupid kids. And I still wasn't sure if he was just toying with me or asking me seriously. Something in my mind told me that he couldn't possibly take me seriously, but something in my heart told me that he and I were all by ourselves, detached from my mother and father and the rest of society, sitting in a quiet, untouched area, speaking intimately and truthfully.

I didn't know the answer. I didn't understand the question. But I knew what to say, and I said it with all the confidence and power that a pubescent, five-foot-five boy could have.

"Yes." I almost shouted it. I was so proud to say it. It felt like one of those self-help seminars, in which the main speaker singles out one helpless person from the crowd and asks them to answer the same question so many times that it eventually turns into a savage chant. Perhaps, that was what he was doing with me. Whether he knew it or not, he had me hung from a piece of string, making me dependent upon his every move. I was torn between gravity and a man I had just met a minute ago.

He chuckled. And, in doing so, let go of the string and dropped me. I was devastated. All my thirteen-year-old's hopes and aspirations rested on his reaction. I had gone all in with that answer, not holding anything back, committed to what laid on the other side. But by the time I got to the other side, I realized that I wasn't ready for it. I regretted my mistake immediately.

"Kid, do yourself a favor." Holding a five-dollar bill in his hand, he said, "Take this and go buy an ice cream." Now I was sure that he was antagonizing me, but I had already gone too far to pack up. I didn't even take the money.

He was laughing at me. My parents were laughing at me. I was so embarrassed that I felt my insides inflame and set fire to everything in my path. He might have been playing games, but he would soon find out that I wasn't. "I don't want your damn ice cream!" I shouted. My parents gasped and Swezey's face straightened.

"Well, what do you want?" Swezey asked.

"I want to make a lot of money, like you," I fired back at him.

"Maybe one day," Swezey said.

"When?" I asked.

He then said something I will never forget, something that tore me up inside for the entire following year, something that served as a great motivation in the future. "When you stop working for money."

I didn't even reply to what he said. Once again, his wording was too vague and underhanded to issue a calm and coherent response. Mr. Swezey made me irregularly uncomfortable. I was used to being the coolest guy in the room, but now, not being first, I was last. All of my swagger had transformed into a shaky mumble and a pair of hunched shoulders.

"Well, I have to get on the road," Mr. Swezey said. "It was nice meeting you two," he said, gesturing to my parents. "I look forward to doing business with you in the near future. You have my card. Call me if you have any questions." He then turned to me and said jokingly, "And for you, Phineas, best of luck in the future. Maybe one day, we can work together and make some real money." He smiled and winked at me before starting toward the front door.

Right as he was reaching for the doorknob, I yelled out to him, "Call me Feeney."

He turned around slowly, made clear, pronounced eye contact with me, and nodded. His classic, devastating smile returned to his face. He then left as he came, suddenly and powerfully.

After Swezey was gone, my dad got up from the table and put his arm around me. "Stay away from that guy. He's a businessman. You can't always trust them."

I just nodded him off me and went to the bathroom to splash some water on my face. Staring up at the mirror, I looked at myself. What made me any different from Mr. Swezey? His clothes, his hair, his jewelry, his car, his demeanor could all be bought. He wore a shell that I had yet to find, but that didn't mean that I couldn't find it one day. He didn't give me a map, but he at least gave me a direction, one opposite from the path I was currently on. That day, I stopped my cigarette sales. I was once again un-self-employed, but this time, I was not desperate to return to work. Work was exactly what I needed to avoid.

I walked out of the bathroom and checked to see if my parents were still in the dining room. They weren't, so I proceeded to grab Mr. Swezey's business card off the table and run upstairs. I entered my bedroom, closed the door behind me, and placed the card underneath my mattress. I lay down, contemplating what Mr. Swezey had said, what my dad had said, and what I had seen in the mirror.

5

Swezey's notion of not working for money didn't resonate well with me until I was fourteen years old. I didn't
know if it meant stealing or hiring other people to do
my work or continuing all my little scams. Lord knows I
never worked too much in comparison to what I pulled
in. Regardless, I dedicated all my time to thinking. The
war was now being fought on a mental front, and that's
where it would forever remain.

My most satisfying attempt came on a Wednesday
afternoon toward the end of the school year. I had blown
off school, taking the bus and then escaping through the
woods. There was a pretty busy town nearby the school
where I figured I would just hang out and look for some
inspiration. I sat down on a bench and waited there for
about two hours. It was so serene, so simple. My head
was clear.

I was sitting across from a decently large bank. The
entire exterior, except for some metal supports, was
glass, a clear window into riches, a transparent medium
through which the power from within could be felt on
the outside. The sunlight reflected perfectly off the windows, illuminating the interior as well as the landscape.

Adorned with beautiful bushes and plants along the perimeter, the building was very pleasing to the eye. And most beautiful of all was the thought of what rested inside.

Kids, parents, and senior citizens were all represented among the people entering the building. Money had a spell on every one of them. All of them needed to feel the extra joy of counting money on the way out of the bank. It was a source of reassurance, of security. We are tied to the green in our pockets. It is an addiction that we all thrive from, some more than most. Why would you walk around with your pockets empty if you didn't have to? I couldn't come up with a reason.

I stood up, walked across the street, and entered the bank. I was blasted with a sensation of cool air and crisp scents. Everybody was scattered about, minding their own business, working as one easygoing, collective unit. ATMs laced the walls, each one separated by a fixed distance. There were several cubicles to both the left and right of the entrance. There was one island in the middle of the bank as well as one long counter directly behind it with all the bankers. In the back was the manager's secluded glass office.

I waited on line for the main counter. It was one of those curly, multidirectional queues organized by ropes. I waited for about ten minutes before getting to the front. The employee, a young, dainty, kind-eyed blonde named Rachel, looked at me with a perplexed expression on her face. After all, I was the youngest person in the bank, besides the babies in the strollers with their mothers.

"Can I help you with something?" she said and smiled.

"Yeah," I said. "Would you mind if I spoke to the manager quickly?"

Squinting her eyes and crunching her face, she replied to the best of her ability.

"Well, I mean, I don't know. What do you have to speak to him about? Do you know him?"

"I'm here to ask about a job. Well, kind of. I have to talk to him. No one else can help me except him."

"I'm sorry, but I really can't let you do that unless you have some type of appointment." I felt bad for her. She was just trying to do her job, and she had some little kid busting her chops. And in addition to that, there was a grumbling line of people behind me that was losing patience by the second.

"But..."

"I'm sorry. You have to leave."

"I'm not leaving." By now, every bystander on line was eavesdropping and felt it was within their rights to join the conversation.

"C'mon, kid," said an older man with patchy brown hair wearing standard business attire.

"All I need is one minute of your manager's time," I replied. "I'm not trying to start a scene."

Another man shouted from the back of the line, "Move your fucking ass, kid!"

Now, I was beginning to start a bit of a commotion. I saw the two bank security guards walking over toward the counter area. I was going to get kicked out anyway, so I figured I would leave a trail of bread crumbs to commemorate my presence.

"I'm not leaving until I speak to a manager!" I yelled at the girl behind the counter and even turned around to address the mob forming behind me. "All of you can shut up. I don't see why this is such a goddamn problem!"

Those comments ensued a mass moaning and groaning from the crowd. The once quiet, tranquil bank now bustled like the New York Stock Exchange. I was the center of attention. And regardless of the circumstances, I was enjoying myself.

However, it didn't take long for me to be yanked out of such enjoyment by Rocco and Rocco. The two security guards both had an arm of mine, and they weren't necessarily being gentle. They just kept repeating, "C'mon, let's go," and, "All right buddy, that's enough." The once angry mob began cheering and clapping in collective pleasure.

By the time the Roccos and I had cleared the counter area, I heard a very authoritative voice shout, "What is going on out here?" The security guards stopped forcing me outside, and all the employees stopped working. Finally, I had gotten my wish. It was the bank manager.

No one answered the manager at first. The entire bank seemed nervous.

The female clerk I had been talking to earlier then walked out from behind the counter. She pulled the manager aside. After about fifteen seconds of whispers, the manager gestured for me to join him in his office. He said, "Let go of him," to the two security guards.

I was sitting down in the office before the manager had even gotten there. He had to talk to a couple more of the employees briefly before addressing the root of the problem. He then entered the room and closed the door.

"You have sixty seconds," said the bank manager while he was walking to his desk. He sat down, looked at his watch, and said, "Go."

Now, I had to issue an apology as well as my original request. "Well, first off, I'm very sorry for causing problems in your bank. All I wanted to ask you was if I could wash your windows for the month."

On the verge of breaking out into hysterical laughter, the manager said, "Are you serious?"

"Yeah," I said and returned his lighthearted smile.

"Well, we already have professionals who do that."

"But I will do it for a billionth of the price."

The manager paused and watched me carefully. "You live around here?"

"Yeah," I lied.

"You have a lawn mower?"

"Yeah," I said, lying again.

"How about you mow the lawn, wash the windows, and just clean up outside every day, and I'll give you one hundred dollars for the month."

I nodded my head slowly.

"Write down your name, number, and address so I can contact you if anything changes." Then the phone rang, making it impossible for me to negotiate. He slid a small notepad toward me.

It was a terrible deal, but it didn't matter to me. If this guy thought I was coming in to work for three dollars a day, he was crazy. I wrote down some bullshit information and went to walk out, only saying, "Thanks, see you tomorrow." But as I reached for the door, the manager stopped me.

He was still on the phone, but now he was thumbing through his wallet. He pulled out a one-hundred-dollar bill and held it out in between his pointer and middle finger.

I was kind of startled by the gesture. Obviously, this was the original plan, but I didn't expect it to unfold as it did. To be honest, I had never even held a one-hundred-dollar bill before. I had often imagined how it would feel, how it would make me feel. I had dreamed of it all before, but now that it was coming to fruition, I have to say that it was a pretty special moment.

I took the money from his fingers and quickly walked out, never to return. Technically, I robbed a bank at the age of fourteen.

I had finally made money without working for it. It was a scam, but it worked. I understood how and why it worked. I understood where it started and where it could take me in the future. Where it would take me in the future.

I marched home with a strong sense of accomplishment and vitality. The amount of money didn't mean all that much to me, but the milestone did. The success of the mission didn't matter all that much either, but the lesson did. I finally had a next step.

I was the man that Swezey had told me to become. It was time to reconnect with him and prove my worth. When I got home, I ran up to my room, grabbed his business card from under my bed, and walked to the nearest train station. I used the one-hundred-dollar bill to buy a ticket into the city.

Before handing me the ticket, the cashier held the one-hundred-dollar bill up to the ceiling light to make sure it was real.

6

I took the 12:30 p.m. train into the city. I sat alone, staring out the window at the passing infrastructure. The
factories, the stores, the houses, the bystanders, the
graffiti all whispered to me. I knew I was headed in the
right direction. The train ride was only twenty minutes
long. It made me wonder why I didn't go to the city
more often.

My parents had always resented what the city stood
for. They were simple people who would much rather
sit quietly by themselves in a backyard than look out
their window to millions of scurrying ants below. The
bustle struck fear into them and the hustle disappointed
their morals. They were happy to live their typical
lives in their typical home in their typical town. They
brought meaning to the word *average* and didn't realize
the curse of their complacency. Their furniture store
kept them just hanging onto the surface, barely floating
under calm and perfect circumstances. Perhaps that is
why they needed Mr. Swezey.

I had always resented what my parents stood for. I
sought to be extraordinary, unique, different. I wanted to
be everywhere, not locked down by an insurmountable

heap of liabilities. When I saw Swezey, I saw all that I had envisioned myself to one day achieve. I was sold on a lifestyle that I knew nothing about. Just jumping on that train, I was sold on a city that I knew nothing about. Yes, I may have been a bit naive. But I had the enthusiasm and dedication to do anything. All I needed was some guidance. Perhaps that is why I needed Swezey.

When I stepped off the train, I saw a new depth of life that I had never experienced before. I was underground, trapped in a dirty, deteriorating dungeon filled with raggedy derelicts and uniformed men with guns. It was quite a transition from my good ole, small American town. I froze briefly after exiting the train and tiptoed away from the platform. I was reduced to a quivering sack of flesh and worries. Real life had slapped me in the face.

I walked hesitantly through the bottom level, trying not to make eye contact with any seated vagrants. Not only was I all alone, but I had a childhood fortune stuffed in my pocket. There was no way for anybody to know that, but in my head, everybody must have. I was a paranoid mess inside, full of unstable, volatile anxieties flying around and colliding with one another. On the surface, I must have seemed petrified.

I made it through the platform level and up the stairs to the remainder of the train station. The conditions did not improve much, but at least there were a lot more people around. I knew that if I ever felt in real danger, I could scream and summon an army of hundreds to save me.

Once I was thrown into the flow of traffic, my worries began to subside. There wasn't time to think. I could only walk. There was nowhere for me to go but straight ahead. I was boxed in on every side by busy, serious-looking adults. The slightest misstep would lead to me being trampled and crushed under the dress shoes of hundreds.

In no time, I was on the outside, sound as a bell. All my fears held no substance. I was overcautious for no one's benefit. I had to let go. I took a deep breath and started my way down 34th Street.

On my journey, I never once looked directly ahead of myself. My eyes were either up in the skyscrapers, among the honks and screeches of traffic, down in the cracks of the sidewalk, or in the minds of the intriguing people passing by. There was so much to take in, and I couldn't walk slowly enough. These were my streets, and one day, everyone would know it.

Everything in the city reminded me of money. The nonstop movement, the struggle just to get down the block, the openhanded beggars on the streets, the sharp sounds of success and failure around every corner, the strength of every piece of infrastructure all tied back to my endless, lucrative cravings. I didn't just see reminders, either. I saw opportunities.

It wasn't long until I was standing before the greatest opportunity of all, Mr. Swezey's office. It had been a twenty-minute walk, but it didn't seem like it. I had to make a million different turns to get there, but I couldn't recall one. I was convinced that I could have walked in any direction I wanted and still would have ended up in the same place.

The office building appeared to be nothing special from the outside. It was tall and narrow, a mere section of a much larger complex of buildings. Aside the door and screwed into the brick was a plastic case holding a piece of paper. The paper detailed the offices represented on each floor. Right at the bottom of the list but at the top of the building was Mr. Swezey's name. Thirty-seventh floor: Swezey Co.

I walked through the door and was greeted with a very bright, clean waiting room. There was one secretary sitting behind a bulky fortress of a desk and four tasteful plastic chairs in a row against a wall. The walls were a bright white. The paint shined, and the marble tile floor was slick and sparkled. The ceiling tiles were made of a glossy blend and the large ceiling lights illuminated the room perfectly. The entire waiting room smelled like peppermint. I loved it, but the secretary didn't seem too happy to be there.

The secretary was pale, bitter, and unenthusiastic. She wore glasses and had straight, dreary brown hair. She had freckles dispersed all over her face and neck. She wore a red sweater with a charm necklace that I could not derive the significance of. The nameplate on her desk read "Joy." Even her voice was bitchy.

"Can I help you?" she asked.

"I'm here to see Mr. Swezey," I said.

"And you are?"

"I'm Michael Ward." That was my father's name. This time, I wasn't going to rely on luck or my fourteen-year-old cuteness. This was serious. I needed to lie like a real man.

Not replying to my statement, the secretary snottily picked up the phone, dialed a few numbers, and said,

"Michael Ward is here to see Mr. Swezey." It took about twenty seconds of her sitting on the phone and twirling her hair before I got the okay to head up the elevator.

I said, "Thank you," and quickly made my way up. I was very excited to finally sit down with Mr. Swezey and speak business. I was nervous, but not in a debilitating way. Thirty-seven floors later, I was breathing a little bit heavy. My heart, on the other hand, was about to burst out of my chest.

I exited the elevator, unknowing of what I was walking into. I planted my feet upon a marble floor and was immediately dwarfed by a giant glass wall. The wall then parted for me, one side to the east and the other to the west. In between was my invitation. The path seemed to illuminate and welcome me in. I was drawn in hopelessly by the light on the other side.

Compared to the first floor, the thirty-seventh could have very well been the lost city of Atlantis. It was immaculate. With its modern, white structure and furniture, the room was surgically constructed to awe and impress guests. The couch was sleek, yet appealing and oh so very comfortable. There were boatloads of rich people magazines and fresh green grapes waiting on a coffee table. The temperature was perfect, just cool enough to be refreshing. It was heaven's waiting room. And God's most beloved angel was at the helm.

Behind a large, beautiful desk sat a woman larger than life and even more beautiful. She had luscious blond hair and gleaming blue eyes and the most supple upturned lips and nose. Her skin was seamless, uniform throughout, and free of fault. Her frame accentuated her surroundings, improving her background with her very shadow on the wall. She was the most beautiful woman I had ever seen, and she wasn't in a magazine or on the big screen or on the Internet. She was a secretary for one man, Mr. Swezey. Her name was Victoria.

"Mr. Ward," she said. "Mr. Swezey should be ready to see you in a few minutes. Sit down."

I couldn't muster even the slightest response. Her grandeur had tied my two lips together. I just smiled and sat down, nearly missing the couch and plopping to the ground. It wasn't my smoothest moment, but I don't think it went as bad as it sounds.

I looked out to the floor as a whole. It was vast and still. Aside from the waiting room and one large office all the way in the back, there was not one sign of life. Hundreds of empty cubicles and offices and computers haunted the area. It seemed like a store past closing, an eerily empty place accustomed to being filled with people.

Appearing like a mansion atop a large, secluded mountain, one trace of life called in the distance. An office the size of a classroom waited at the very edge of the floor, directly above the street. I couldn't make much of what I was seeing, being so far away. But I did see a man. His silhouette seemed to pace back and forth. He was my man, Mr. Swezey.

"Mr. Swezey will see you now," said the secretary.

No, I will see Mr. Swezey now.

7

The thirty-second walk to Mr. Swezey's office told me everything I had to know about what I was getting myself into. The silence grew with every second. I felt my heart beating twice for each step. I wondered where all the other employees had gone or if there even were any other employees. Were the desks there just for show? Did Mr. Swezey really buy out this entire floor just for himself? Before I could answer any questions, I was at the door.

I put myself in Mr. Swezey's shoes. What would he possibly think when I walked through his door? He was expecting my father, an unspectacular visit to begin with. He was probably very busy and wouldn't want to be bothered by any childish games. I hadn't seen the man in nearly a year, and here I was today, uninvited and unwanted. I almost felt bad.

However, there was a chance that Mr. Swezey would be intrigued by my young drive. Perhaps he would appreciate my desire to be in his life and pay my curiosity tenfold. I just wanted to learn. I didn't want any of his money; I wanted his knowledge of how to make money. I was tired of counting by ones, fives, tens, and twenties.

I had reached the second level but couldn't pick myself off the floor. I needed someone to raise me up so I could continue along my journey to the top.

The moment the door opened, Mr. Swezey's eyes hit me. He was sitting down at an extravagant desk, pen in hand, evidently busy with something. Behind him was a glass window displaying an iconic view of a park, a lake, and the tops of the city's most prominent skyscrapers. It all struck my blood cold. Mr. Swezey's immediate expression was of surprise, but he easily adapted to the situation and issued me a greeting.

"Feeney," Mr. Swezey said. He grinned, almost as if he were expecting me.

Taken back by his readiness, I started. "Hey, Mr. Swezey—"

"Did I call you Phineas?" he interrupted, smiling at me and pausing briefly. "It's Swezey." He stood up and walked around the desk to a nearby counter. On the counter, there were short, wide glasses, a bucket of ice, and a cut glass bottle of scotch. Swezey poured two glasses.

"Sorry. Sw—"

Interrupting me again, Swezey said, "Don't apologize. Have a drink."

Hardly comprehending what was going on, I said, "A drink?"

He approached me purposefully. "Only the best of the best, Feeney." He basically threw the half-filled glass at me. If I had been the slightest bit hesitant in reaching, it would have fallen to the floor and shattered. "Take a seat." He then walked back around his desk and sat down. I followed, now sitting in a sophisticated brown leather chair.

Here I was, fourteen years old, sitting in a random top-floor city office with a rich psychopath, scotch in hand. I was terrified. I had never drunk before, not even champagne at a wedding. Now, I was expected to guzzle liquor that I had only heard of in movies. He handed it to me like it was a water bottle. I couldn't turn him down, but I couldn't bring myself to drink it, either. It felt heavy in my hands, and the smell stung my nostrils.

Swezey was staring at me from his chair. He had a serious expression on his face and paused for about five seconds. He then smirked and slowly raised his glass to his lips. He drank and lowered it down to the wood of his desk. He had held eye contact the entire time.

I felt pressure from all angles. I had to man up. Against the wishes of every adult I had ever met up until that point, I took a sip. I felt a ball of fire cascade down my esophagus and all the way through to my stomach, scorching every stretch of its path. My eyes squinted and my mouth fought for its life as I frantically shook my head in bodily shock. When my nervous system recovered and my eyes opened, I saw Swezey smiling from ear to ear in amusement. Raising up his glass again, Swezey said, "So talk to me." He took another sip.

I was still a little dazed by the power of the scotch. I was even more dumbfounded as to how Swezey was drinking it so easily. It wasn't in any way unpleasant to him. In fact, it seemed refreshing. Figuring it would be better the second time, I took another sip. It wasn't.

Swezey was patient with me but clearly wanted to get to the point. I gathered myself and started. "I've been thinking about what you said last time we met, about not working for money." I spoke gently, not wanting to impose.

Swezey looked at me very critically and paused, probably trying to remember exactly what he had said to me. He took another sip of his scotch and said, "Go on."

I told him the story about how I had met with the manager of the bank, promised my services, and took his money up front. I told him about the one-hundred-dollar bill. I even told him about all the stuff I used to do to make money, from picking flowers to selling cigarettes. Swezey sat and listened patiently, never interrupting or losing focus.

Swezey got up from his chair, scotch still in his right hand, and walked over to the window behind him. He leaned against it with his left shoulder, tucked his left hand in his pocket, and looked out. Without regaining eye contact, he said, "Tell me Feeney. What do you love?"

"What do I love?" I repeated, truly asking myself the question. I didn't know what to say. I guess I had never been asked that question before. I looked down silently, wondering how I could respond.

I then heard a loud crash of glass, a smack of wood, and a furious man yell, "Why are you here, Phineas?" Swezey had lost his shit. He had thrown his glass against the wall to my left and struck the palms of his hands against the desk. I looked up to see his demonic eyes flaring at me. He had a crazed look on his face and nothing but anger behind it. And to think he was peacefully looking out his window just a few seconds ago.

Scared to death, I muttered, "Uh, I don't, uh—"

"Why are you here?" he yelled again. Swezey was not playing with me anymore. He wanted an answer, and he wanted it now. Without time to think, a response shot out of me.

"I want to make money!" I screamed at him. I was now as angry as he was. My breath was heavy and my heart was racing. And as a result, he got the truth.

Swezey smiled at me, took a step back, and said, "Ah, so you love money." His voice had changed from militant and psychotic to elongated and sarcastic. He sat back down in great joy.

This guy was fucking nuts! I couldn't believe what had just happened. I was so angry that I couldn't bear to muster up a response. I was one word from flying over the desk and killing him.

Now serious again, Swezey said, "I want you back here tomorrow at nine. Wear your nicest clothes and bring all your money." Swezey was done talking to me.

I didn't argue. I had nothing left in me to argue. I was exhausted and glad the whole thing was over. "I'll see you tomorrow, Swezey."

I walked out the door. I said good-bye to the secretary, took the elevator down to the lobby, and made my way back to the train station. This time through the city was not nearly as dramatic. I was only focused on tomorrow.

When I arrived home much later that night, both my parents were sitting on the couch, arms and legs crossed, waiting for me. They were not only pissed, but deeply worried. They had gotten a call from the school notifying them that I wasn't in attendance. They then called all my friends' parents to see if their sons had also cut or if I was with them. Nobody knew where I had gone. They were minutes from calling the police when I walked through the door.

"Where the hell were you?" my mother shouted and stood up. "You had us worried sick."

"I went to the city," I said.

"The city? For what?" She was still shouting. My dad stood next to her silently, maintaining a very serious facial expression.

"I just wanted to go to the city," I lied.

"Are you serious?" I had never seen my mother so angry. "I can barely even look at you right now. What has gotten into you lately? Every day, it's something else."

"I'm sorry." I calmly walked past them and toward the stairs. My parents didn't know how to react. My lack of empathy and concern made it impossible for them to effectively punish me.

"Where do you think you're going?" They had both turned around to face me, but my mother was still the only one speaking. "Do you have any idea how much trouble you're in?"

"I'm really tired. I'm going to bed. Good night." And that's what I did. I entertained no further questions and refused to give them the time of day. I walked up the stairs, entered my bedroom, and closed the door. I took all the money remaining from the one-hundred-dollar bill, stored it in my backpack, and went to sleep.

8

The next morning, I thought about how angry my mother was the previous night. I had deceived her trust, ripping it from her very hands and crushing it beneath my feet. I had traumatized her, leaving her with the notion that her only beloved son could have been injured, kidnapped, or murdered. I had broken her heart, not even acknowledging her plight and throwing her aside like a used tissue. And the worst part of all, I was going to do it all over again.

Luckily, there were only a few more days of school at that point, so I wouldn't have to hurt my mother much more. But on that day, I had no choice. I didn't know what Mr. Swezey wanted with me. I didn't know if he was aware of the schism that was likely to occur between me and my family. I barely even knew who Mr. Swezey was. However, my priorities were set a long time ago, back when I had sold all my parents' belongings on their own front lawn. Money ruled all, and family fell in comparison.

When I came downstairs at 6:40 a.m. to eat breakfast and get ready for *school*, my mother was waiting at the dining table. Usually, she was gone by then, prepping the store for the day and filling out paperwork from 7:00 a.m. to 2:00 p.m. That way, she could see me get off the bus. My dad normally woke up around 7:00 a.m. to make sure I got on the bus.

"Good morning, Feeney," my mother said, looking up lovingly with a cup of coffee resting in her right hand.

"Hi, Mom," I replied. It was a pretty awkward greeting. Given how I had treated her, I didn't know if she had any underlying motives beneath her amiable exterior. Normally, she wouldn't say a word to me. I was nervous to say the least, worried by her forgiveness and warmth. "Shouldn't you be getting to work soon?" Her shoes weren't on yet.

"No," she said. "I took off work today. I figured we could spend the day together. I was going to call the school now." This was a nightmare.

"Mom, it's really okay. You don't have to."

"But I want to. We haven't spent a day together in forever."

"I really have to go to school though. I already missed yesterday." I basically vomited those words out of my mouth.

"Don't worry. One more day won't hurt."

"I have too many tests today, Mom. I really can't."

"We can go out for lunch and go into town. I have to go to the bank first." Just when I thought it couldn't get any worse.

"Mom, I'm serious. I really need to go to school." What kind of human being was I? My sweet, merciful, and tender mother sacrificed her time and responsibilities to share an afternoon with me, and I chose to lie just to avoid her. All she wanted was her son back. It was as if she knew that the end was in sight. She reached her arm out one last time to save me, but I didn't do the same.

Dejected and visibly sad, my mother said, "Okay, Feeney, but at least let me drive you to school." This notion threw another wrench into my original plan, but looking at my mother's drooping face, I couldn't reject her again.

"Sure, Mom. That sounds great," I lied. At the time, I didn't realize how terrible my actions were. I was selfish and stupid. All I cared about was myself. I saw my parents as obstacles that only made things more difficult.

Not having to take the bus any longer, I ate breakfast quickly and fell back asleep on the couch for a half hour. My mother woke me up again at 7:10 a.m. to get in the car. Before leaving, I made sure to fill my backpack with a dress shirt, a tie, a belt, and a pair of dress pants and shoes. I also ran around to the back and collected my entire life savings from under the deck.

It was a quiet ride. I didn't want to say anything, and my mother didn't know how to handle my silence. I felt guilty about what I would soon do, but not enough to stop myself.

We arrived at the school around 7:25 a.m., first period started at 7:40 a.m., and the closest train to the city left at 8:00 a.m. I would have to be precise and agile with my actions to successfully pull off the mission.

"Bye. I'll see you later," my mother said.

"Bye," I said lifelessly. I opened the door, put on my backpack, and exited the car. As I turned my back, I heard my mother.

"I love you." She said it so profoundly, so deeply that I almost got choked up. After all that I had done to her in such a short amount of time, she still didn't have a resentful bone in her body. My piece of shit self couldn't even muster up the decency to respond. I just sort of nodded and made my way toward the school.

When I got to the doors, I looked back to my mother exiting the parking lot. I pictured her crying, reminiscing of times when I was too young and innocent to hurt anyone's feelings, searching for some mistake she had made to make me who I was. She would likely go home to my father in shambles and bury her distraught face into his chest. He would reassure her that it was just a phase, but worry just as much himself. They carried the same weight, just in different ways.

I waited for five minutes after my mother had left the parking lot. Then, I started my journey toward the train station. I estimated it to be about a twenty-five-minute walk, a twenty-minute hustle. I chose to hustle, for I still needed to get dressed. And considering the fact that my entire future rested on boarding that train, I couldn't afford to gamble.

I slipped out of the lobby in which all the kids congregated before first period. I then ran through the trees on the left flank of the school. It was both a shortcut and a way to avoid being detected by any tattletales or nosy bystanders.

Running through the woods, I felt every essence of nature press upon my body. I felt twigs and pines delicately crunch under the balls of my feet. I felt the morning dew slowly cascade off the tree branches and leaves and down onto my clothed shoulders. It was just a typical wood, but in that moment, it could have been mistaken for the Garden of Eden. Entrenched in the trees and my own temptations, there was no going back. My actions would lead to the undeserved suffering of others.

Eventually, I exited the woods and got to the road. From there, I could just walk or jog in a straight line to the train station. I had a watch so that I could adjust my pace accordingly.

This walk was pretty foreign to me at the time. I had made it only once. I had been in this part of town only a few times to begin with. My parents had always warned me against it, swearing to me that nothing good happened on the other side of the train tracks. It was different, but not foreboding or shady. Everything always sounded worse in my parents' voices. As a result, everything seemed great once I actually experienced it, even when it wasn't.

I reached the train station at 7:52 a.m., bought my ticket, and went to the bathroom to change. I boarded the train, surrounded by countless joyless adults, wearing worn and monotonous business suits. Some would say that I was out of place, but those are the same people whose only source of income when they were my age was taking out the garbage.

As the train was departing, I looked out the window to the parking lot. Parked on the opposite side of the lot was my mother's car. It wasn't actually her car, but an identical model. It reminded me of what I was doing and how there was no second chance from here. I was on my way to a new life, apart from the past and resentful of my roots.

I was finally alone and all grown up, dressed in a cheap suit, on a train to my place of work in the city, reminiscing of the old days, and saying good-bye to a prior way of living. I was fourteen years old.

9

I arrived at Mr. Swezey's office at 8:50 a.m. I waited for fifteen minutes. In that period of time, my mind jumped to all four corners of the map. Perhaps he was avoiding me or out of town or sick or hurt or dead. I was paranoid in anticipation for what would possibly never come. I sat boiling in my seat in contrast to the icy chillness of the silent princess before me. I felt the temptation to bolt out of the waiting room and sit alone on the staircase. I regretted all my lies and tricks and cheats. All they had done was suspend me over a cliff.

I heard a beep from the elevator. With it, my heart fell into my stomach. The sound rang through my ears, rattled around my brain, and reverberated down my spinal cord, sending chills throughout every stretch of my muscle tissue. I assumed it to be Arthur Swezey, but my pessimistic mindset promised me otherwise.

When Mr. Swezey revealed himself, he darted right over to me, shook my hand, and said, "Let's get after it." He proceeded to greet the secretary and take a handful of envelopes from her hand. Never slowing down, he glided into his office while I tried to keep up.

When we entered his office, he instructed me to close the door and sit down. I put my backpack down at my feet. He was scurrying around his office, peaking into a file cabinet on one side and then quickly jumping to the other to pour himself a glass of scotch. He took one sip and returned to the other side of the room.

"How long ago did you get here?" he asked me, thumbing through a bunch of files and not making eye contact. He was such a focused multitasker. Although it didn't seem it based on his body language, I knew that he was giving me all the attention I needed.

"Like fifteen minutes," I said.

"Now tell me," he said, "why would you ever think it was a good idea to be anywhere ten minutes early?" He finally looked up at me.

"Um, I don't know. Isn't that what you're supposed to do?" I was accustomed to custom. I had no personal reasoning behind my actions, and Swezey saw right through it.

"What use are those ten minutes when you are sitting down doing nothing but waiting for something that may never come? You probably even got nervous." He now leaned on his desk facing me, piercing into me with his sharp blue eyes.

"I guess, a little." It made sense.

"By arriving slightly late, you don't allow yourself to get nervous and you build anticipation for your arrival. Tell me honestly, how relieved were you when you heard the elevator?" He was going off, one point after the other, each one stronger than the prior.

"I—I was happy," I said, laughing. A smile came over me in fascination and impression, but he wasn't close to done.

"Did you bring the money like I told you?" His tone changed, but I still knew that a flip was in sight.

"Yeah." I answered with a great deal of reluctance.

"How much?"

"I don't know. Around ninety-five hundred."

"Is that all of it?"

"Basically." I still didn't know what he was getting at.

"First off, why would you ever tell me how much money you have on you? And why would you ever, ever, ever carry all of your money around with you?" He almost seemed angry.

"You told me to," I said, raising my voice at him slightly.

He then snatched my backpack out from underneath me and threw it out an open window behind him. I screamed like a little girl. My heart stopped and my stomach dropped. Tears began to materialize in my eyes.

"See what just happened," he said. "That's why you never tell ANYONE ANYTHING about how much money you have. And that is why we don't play with cash unless we know exactly what we are doing with it." His eyes were as serious as I had ever seen. I was petrified of what I had gotten myself into.

I didn't respond. I couldn't. All I had worked for, all I had sacrificed was now flung onto the city streets, unprotected and unlikely to ever return.

"Now," he began, "why would you risk losing all your money just to be an extra ten minutes early? Wherever you go, you're in and you're out. There is no waiting around for anything." He was forceful in his preaching.

I could only nod in response. My face was stricken in shock and dismay. I must've looked like a basset hound that was stuck in the heat for too long, cheeks drooping, ears flailing, world ending. Mr. Swezey smiled at me.

He then walked around to the other side of his desk, opened up a little drawer, and pulled out a huge stack of one-hundred-dollar bills wrapped in a rubber band. "Consider this your first lesson." He shook the stack right by his head. "Obviously, I'm not going to make you pay ninety-five hundred bucks per lesson." He tossed me the money. It was ten thousand dollars. I almost fainted again. "Keep the change."

Looking at the money, I just chuckled and grinned. "What's the next lesson?" I joked. Smiling, he approached me and shook my hand.

"Welcome to Swezey Co."

From there, he went on to tell me all about himself. He told me about how he was a hotshot broker at the age of twenty-five for a big-time firm in the city and how he quit after having some issues with management. He told me about how corrupt all the major brokerage firms were and about all the illegal activity they frequently participated in. He discussed with me why he chose to open up his own little investment company rather than take further part in the criminality of mainstream business. He made it seem like he already had all the money he needed and that his current work was just to help and look out for people in need. Mr. Swezey was the man. He had life by the balls. He was my idol, and now my mentor.

I stayed in his office until 6:30 p.m. He introduced me to the basics of the stock market, the principles of investing, and the foundation of money management. I learned more in that afternoon than I ever did in school. All the concepts were geared on money, and therefore resonated deeply within my psyche and attitude. There were no notes or PowerPoint presentations or dittos. We just talked for hours. He asked me questions not to see if I knew the answers, but because he was genuinely interested in what I had to say. However, it couldn't go on all day.

"Sorry, Feeney," he said, "but I have a meeting. I gotta go. You can come if you want." I couldn't tell if he actually wanted me to come or if he was just saying that.

Looking down at my watch, I didn't know where the time had gone. I had to get home, if I still had a home. "No, it's okay," I said. "I really have to get home."

"Okay, I'll see you tomorrow, same time." He said it without any idea of what I had given up to get there the previous two days. It was as if he knew I would come no matter what. As insensitive as it was, he was right.

"See you tomorrow. Thanks for everything." Swezey smiled and nodded and saw me on my way out.

When we split paths, I looked back at him. He was so cool. The sway with which he walked, the way he carried his head above his shoulders, the way his feet seemed to never make contact with the ground was so transcendent of all his peers. He strolled into the setting sun, illuminating himself with flowing shades of orange and amber, red and yellow. He was not from a world I was used to living in. My world awaited me, and considering the vibrancy I had witnessed all day, it was going to be darker than ever.

It was about 8:00 p.m. when I had reached my door. I looked through the window and saw my mother lounging on a recliner without a speck of life on her face. She sat with her legs together, slanted to the left side of her body and resting on the chair. Her eyes were absorbed by some television program, but her mind was elsewhere.

I entered through the door and awkwardly greeted my mother. "Hi, Mom." She didn't even acknowledge my presence. I stood at the front door mat for a few seconds, waiting for a reply that was nowhere in sight. When I realized that I was alone, I dropped my head and walked upstairs. Halfway up the stairs, I said, "I'm sorry." Once again, her head didn't budge. I had broken her. I walked the rest of the way up and into my room. I had always rejoiced in having an empty house, but not this one.

Sitting in my room, I listened for any sign of life. Before long, I heard sniffling and squeaking and eventually weeping. My mother was gone. She was now just a woman who lived with me and cooked me dinner and cleaned my stuff. Our natal and emotional connection was reduced to a burden that had to be eliminated. And it was. Instead of fighting to retain it, I found it elsewhere, in Swezey. And every time I sought to empower that new connection, the older one became more and more distant.

Eventually, the past would be a sea away, cloaked in a thick, amorphous layer of fog, void of sunlight. I would push away from it, never thinking to return, forgetting what I left on the other side.

10

I never had to deal with my mother taking off work again. I never had to sneak away again. I never had to worry about coming home to yells and screams and punishments again. I had broken through the first line of defense and, despite taking heavy casualties, was in the clear from then on. Whether the juice was worth the squeeze did not matter in my young mind.

The school year had just ended, and my summer was booked, not with ball games and beach days, but with long hours of tangible education. I was enrolled in a summer school of one. Everyone else had to suffer the toil of being normal.

Every day, I entered through Swezey Co.'s doors bigger and stronger than the day before. I felt better and therefore performed better each and every day. I saw new things, met new people, and introduced myself to new, previously unknown parts of my own self. I changed while all my contemporaries relished in staying the same and relaxing during their time off. But I guess you could say that there are two types of people in this world.

Every day was a lesson of a different sort. Some came in the shape of my first lesson, built into conversation and extracted from misunderstanding. Others came in more of a classroom setting style. He would drill an idea into my head mercilessly, cementing it over until not an ounce of information could leak out. There were also some lessons that Swezey would bring about from his observations of other people. He pinpointed their mistakes and guaranteed that I would never repeat them myself. No matter the medium of education, each lesson was heeded with particular intensity and passion. It felt good to actually learn something.

One day, I came to work without a suit jacket. I had spilt mustard on it the night before, and I only had one. I brought it into the Laundromat before work one morning, not thinking it to be a big deal. I was still wearing a nice shirt and tie and dress pants. Most of the time, we just stayed in the office anyway. My jacket was on the back of a chair more often than it was on me.

I walked into Swezey's office feeling a little bit guilty, but not enough apparently. The moment he saw me, his hands flew up to his sides. "What the hell, Feeney?"

Exposed and truly feeling naked now, I said, "Yeah, I'm sorry, Swezey. I got mustard—"

"Mustard?" he interrupted. "Listen, Feeney, I don't care. You don't have to say sorry or make any excuses or anything. It's perfectly fine. I'm just kidding."

"Really? Okay." I paused. "So what are we doing today?" I didn't see that coming. I thought I was about to get a whole big preach about professionalism and all that bullshit, but I guess not.

"I don't know, man. What do you want to do?" he said with a huge, fake, gaudy smile on his face. I didn't even respond. I knew he was fucking with me now.

He continued, "How about we send pictures of our dicks to all our clients and see if that helps us close some deals?" His voice moved in a perfect crescendo, getting louder with each word up until the point when he was actually screaming. He was not done.

He went on, "How about we ditch the dress shirts and just start wearing suspenders? But covering the nipples, of course. Very tasteful." Although I knew I was being scolded, I couldn't stop laughing.

Once again, he continued, "Do you know why we don't have casual Friday, Feeney?" This actually sounded like a real question, so I decided to add some comic relief of my own.

"Um, because you only have two employees."

He didn't react to my joke. He clearly had a point to prove. "Don't you think I would love seeing Victoria over there wearing a tank top and miniskirt?" He bit his fist at me in frustration. "Oh, trust me, I would. But would you give your hard-earned money to somebody who looks like they just got off their shift at the strip club?" He paused and looked at me, not to answer, but for dramatic effect. He continued.

"A person is only going to trust you if they think that you are better than them. And that starts with appearance. I understand that it was only a suit jacket, but what if your client was wearing a suit jacket? They would win, and you would lose. We have to dominate on all fronts. Do you see what I'm saying?"

He was right. I couldn't say anything in rebuttal. I just nodded and smiled and said, "Yes. Yes, I do."

"Good." He then handed me five hundred dollars and told me to head down the block and buy the nicest suit I could find. He taught me everything I needed to do and gave me everything I needed to do it. He considered me to be an extension of himself, and he was not going to be embarrassed, not even by the slightest flaw.

Swezey taught me a new way of living, of talking, of walking, of winning. Although I didn't get paid at all that summer, I felt as if I had. The joy and power I felt on a daily basis far exceeded anything I had ever experienced before. It was the feeling that I had always been chasing. It was what I had in my mind every time I had organized a scheme, except I had always fallen short then. Now, I stood atop a mountain, looking down upon my path, still just at the beginning of my journey.

It was now that Swezey told me what I would be doing for him. I was going to be selling investment pitches to clients of his choice. I would study potential investment opportunities, visit people, and sell them on the program. Once I retrieved their principal investment, I would hand the money over to Swezey and be on to the next one. I was a high-stakes traveling salesman. Everything else about the process was out of hand, sight, and mind. I had one thing to master and a whole summer to master it.

He taught me the art of the sale. He emphasized the idea of knowing your shit frontward and backward and leftward and rightward. Nobody wants to deal with an amateur. They want facts in confidence, no guesswork or variables. I saw this as the most crucial part of my job and refused to allow it to be my downfall. Now, my day didn't end when I left the office. I was bringing my work home with me, spending long nights mastering every last nook and cranny of each opportunity. Before long, I knew more about them than Swezey did.

I even studied my clients. I did hours of research every night before a sale. I knew what they did for a living, what kind of a car they drove, how many kids they had, how much they bought their house for, everything. I knew exactly what buttons to push to make my clients fall to their knees. They saw me as a very personal salesman. Little did they know, I was just ahead of the game.

Timing was also a pivotal part of the process. Any amount of knowledge can be made useless if accessed at the wrong time. Any opportunity can seem worthless if opened for too long or closed too early. The minute I got a favorable reaction, I was taught to get in and get out. A yes was a yes, and the only thing it could change to from there was a no. We weren't in the business of convincing and changing people's minds. We were out to find the tiny voices in people's minds that agreed with us. Before long, all doubts would be drowned out. If not, we walked away.

For this reason, I was told to only take cash and checks. I refused all credit and favors and bargains. You either had it or you didn't. I wasn't the type to wait, and if you kept me waiting for money, you had already lost my business. The policy was strong. I was never paid in cash though, only checks. It made sense. Who would trust a kid with cash?

Another pillar of the system was keeping on the fine line between familiarity and detachment. I had to become best friends with the client to their face, but complete strangers behind the scenes. They needed to trust me, but I still had to lie to them about every aspect of my life. All relationships were to end the minute I turned my back or hung up. I remember the first time Swezey told me about this concept.

"Feeney, what's your phone number?" he asked. I didn't know why he asked. I talked to him on the phone more than anyone else. But I played along anyway.

"Six-three-one five-five-nine five-seven-four two," I replied. "Why?"

"Well, here's your new phone number," he said, sliding a piece of paper to me.

I looked at him curiously. "What do you mean?"

He slid me another piece of paper and said, "And here's your phone number two months from now."

I sat there, now holding both pieces of paper in my hand. I didn't say anything.

He continued. "What name do you like better—Anthony or Dominic?"

I started laughing. "What are you talking about it?" I kind of shouted.

Apparently, I was to change my phone number every two months and use a different name for every client. I knew how shady it sounded, but it was too much fun being a different person every day. There was never a dull moment at Swezey Co.

I wasn't even allowed to tell anybody where I worked or who I worked for. If any non-client were to ask, I would have to lie and say that I worked in my parents' furniture store. And even with clients, I could never tell them about Mr. Swezey. I was merely an employee, unconnected with corporate leadership, taking orders as they were given.

This way, I was totally protected from any liability. Swezey didn't want me to suffer from the backlash of potential failed investments. I was designed to sail only in calm waters. At the first sign of chop, I was to hand over controls to Swezey. But nothing ever happened. I was too well trained to run blindly into trouble.

Obviously, a salesman is nothing without a golden tongue. Swezey taught me how to twist and sculpt sentences to hit the heart most directly. There was always a perfect way to say something and, with time, I became better at finding that way. Before long, I could say anything in an optimistic, positive tone. The time was always right to strike. Everything was always going as planned. I was always selling the opportunity of a lifetime. It wasn't bullshit. It was just from a different angle.

However, being a teenager, all these tactics alone would never be enough. Who was I to tell grown adults what to do with their money? Most of them had homes and families before I was even born. I was forced to shock and awe. I needed to impress and fool my clientele with illusions of riches, with expensive disguises. At the age of fourteen and with less than ten thousand dollars to my name, I became the lucrative envy of hundreds.

What was Swezey's would become mine. When I was of age, I would borrow his cars, his watches, his clothes, his phones, his homes, his life. I would park in front of my clients' houses in $100,000 cars ten to twenty minutes late. I would slowly exit the car in my $500 sunglasses, adjust my $1,000 suit, and check the time on my $20,000 watch. I flaunted it all right in front of their middle-class faces, triggering the innate human greed lying within their psyches. It wasn't even greed. It was pure jealousy. How would you react if a kid one-third of your age was living your dreams right in front of you?

I would make sure that they knew I was the best of a young, unstoppable generation that they knew nothing about. And the reason I was the best was because of the investments I was selling. First, they would be embarrassed that they were being outpaced by a child. Then, they would be fearful of missing out on the future, of being lapped by others, of losing. It would all end with their desperation, and thus their commitment.

They knew their involvement didn't mean shit to me. Whether they signed or not, I was still leaving their house rich. The only people they were helping or hurting were themselves. They could either stay home or pull alongside next to me in the fast lane to wealth.

I didn't subtly open up that lane, either. I illuminated it with neon lights and unmistakable sounds of raw speed and intensity. I let them know where I was coming from the instant I reached their door. First impressions were chances to push my opposition back on their heels and infiltrate their homes, their livelihoods, and, most importantly, their wallets.

Sometimes, I would approach a new client without even introducing myself and ask, "Do you know how much a million dollars weighs?" The clients would be stunned by my energy and intrusiveness. They would stand, hand outstretched and empty, silent, confused as to who the real adult was in the conversation. The power balance was won.

I would give them a few seconds until I saw the client's lips begin to move. Before they had a chance to say anything, I would fire back at them. "Twenty-two pounds in hundreds." I would pause again, analyzing their countenance for any abrupt changes. "After this investment, you're gonna need a gym membership because YOU WILL be a millionaire, and twenty-two pounds is heavier than you think."

I never found out which of my clients became rich or not. That wasn't my business. I trusted Swezey and his intentions. One day, I asked Swezey if I could invest in what I was selling.

"Why would you ever want to do that, Feeney?" he responded.

"I don't know. I figured that if all these other people are going to make money, why shouldn't I? I mean, I do know everything about all the programs."

He stood up from his desk, somewhat perplexed and taken back. I don't think he had expected such a thought from me. "By investing in what you sell, you become partial. Your job is to be as independent as possible. You don't form relationships, and you don't worry about what happens after the sale is made. This is for your own protection and success."

"Protection from what?" I asked.

"From being overwhelmed. Remember, you're still just a boy."

"But I know this stuff! I've never known anything better in my entire life." My yelling hit Swezey irregularly. He took a step back and looked down for a brief moment.

"How about this?" he said, now looking up. "When you turn eighteen, we will do an investment together. Until then, save up money, have a good time, and stay with your sales. Trust me, it's for the best."

Deflated, I nodded and said, "Okay, Swezey."

The summer flew by, and high school was upon me. However, I wasn't worried about fitting in or my classes or all that basic high school bullshit. All my worries circulated around applying my lessons into action. My training was complete. It was time.

11

The rush of my first sale was unlike anything I had ever experienced before. It made the hair stand up on the back of my neck and arms. I felt as if I had discovered the New World, but this world was not to be shared among an entire nation. It was all mine. And Swezey's. But he already owned a world of his own. Sitting upon his throne, he sent me with the ship and the guns and the flag, but I was the one to set my foot down on fresh soil and yell to the heavens in triumph.

Business boomed. The combination of greed, jealousy, and desperation did our jobs for us. We just had to serve the plate, and it wouldn't be long until the hungry savages in front of us dug in. My training had been flawless and the execution followed. Everything went well, and with time, I began to take on more responsibility. And with me earning 10% commission on each sale, more responsibility was good.

I never really understood the concept of commission in how Swezey Co. worked. Professional Wall Street brokers only made 2%, and they were working for titan brokerages. How could Swezey, one man, afford to give me five times that without any of the qualifications?

Each check was written to Swezey's personal account, and he always gave me my share in straight cash. I didn't understand where the money was coming from. All I knew was that the money was headed directly to my pocket, and that was good enough for me.

At the age of fourteen, I only sold a few investments. Swezey didn't want to overwhelm me, and most of my work was being done on the weekends anyway. I also couldn't drive, and public transportation often made things very difficult. Sometimes, Swezey would even come to the sales with me. I was being molded at a precise and measured pace. I saw all my missions then as scrimmages. The lights would be on soon, and I couldn't afford to waste time being a rookie.

With my next birthday came an increase in hours. I started selling three or four days a week and cutting school regularly. I now had a little bit of capital and many more big names on the schedule. Money started to pile up quickly, but Swezey encouraged me to save it for the time being and not to get too rich too young. By that, he didn't mean not making too much money. He meant not showing my hand when there was still much game to be played.

At sixteen years old, I fell off the wagon. And into a Ferrari tearing down the interstate. Now that I had my driver's permit, Swezey had no problem letting me drive his cars. I was working as much as I could, and I was not wasting my time saving anymore. Money was coming in so fast that I couldn't have stored it all if I tried. I either had to spend it or burn it. So, I burned it on every single thing that caught my eye.

Every once in a while, the stars would align and I would find myself in a classroom, fielding nonsense from teachers about how I was never in school. I didn't fight back. I just took out my keys and started my $100,000 car from my desk.

There were still mistakes at sixteen though. I was a hotshot up-and-comer and not yet the surgical professional that knew his way around the business. By the time I was seventeen, I had developed a system that couldn't be beat. Money flowed like the rivers of ancient Babylon. There were no longer good weeks and bad weeks. They were all just business weeks, and business was always great.

At the peak of my game, Swezey would typically hand me a list of ten residences per day. Out of the ten, I would close three or four. Out of those three or four, the average investment would be about $10,000. So at 10% commission, I was making about $3,500 every fucking day. In case you can't figure it out yourself, that's $17,500 a week, $75,833 a month, $910,000 a year.

I now had my own cars, my own clothes, and my own watches. I had everything a young man could ever want, but most of all, I had freedom. I didn't need school to tell me how to live my life. I didn't need my parents for money, transportation, or even shelter. I was making enough money to buy out the mortgage on my parents' house every six months. The nicest car in our driveway was signed in my name. And I had more money hidden under the deck than my parents had in their retirement fund. I answered to only one man, and as a partner, not a bitch.

Working had built my life, but my life was not built for work. Every day after I had stowed away my day's take and hung up my suit, I would sit at my childhood desk. I would record the names, phone numbers, and addresses of each new client in a tiny, black, leather-bound notebook. When the book shut, work would be over. It was then time to play.

12

I was the fucking man.

Everywhere I went, I knew it and it didn't take everyone else long to find out for themselves. I was living all my classmates' dreams while they were still dreaming them. When I walked, others not only followed, but they cleared a path.

No matter the encounter, I always held the leverage in my pocket. If people were better than me at something, I made sure to let them know that I made more money than their parents. If people insulted me, I made sure to remind them that talk was cheap and they were broke. More than anything else, I loved tearing into adults who thought they had some type of authority over me. Just as I did at work, I made a point of telling them what I was doing and what they were failing to do. I killed the spirits of grown men and grew in spirit with each victim.

The only person I couldn't do that with was Swezey, and that's what made our relationship so unique. I had nothing on him, and he never held anything against me. We both thrived in the balance.

Living the high life, I spent money as it came. I carried thousands of dollars in cash around with me everywhere I went. I only counted the commas on the price tags. If there weren't any, it was immediately mine. If there were, I would give it some thought, and it would eventually become mine. It got to the point where I would run through an entire week's pay in a day. It didn't matter to me though. I rationalized that I would just make it back the next week.

I indulged myself in the gym as well. Every day, I would work out with the sole purpose of being better than everyone else. I would talk shit about all the fat people at the gym, despite having clear, tangible evidence that they were trying to better themselves. I saw everything else as black and white, and myself in vibrant, beautiful color.

My strength also offered me some other privileges of dominance. After all, an asshole wouldn't be a true asshole if he didn't habitually force fights. Now knowing that I would win most fights, I was able to commit to being an asshole that much more. It got to the point that the minute a conflict started to materialize, I was swinging. Before long, people started to pace away from me. Some were afraid. Some just didn't want the aggravation.

I made a point to make my presence noted at all times, so I parked my car in front of everywhere I went. My car was my symbol. Parking tickets came, but I never minded paying them.

To be honest, I can't recall too many good friends I had back then. Even today, I am basically alone. I had business associates and people I frequently partied with, but no true friends. Perhaps I lived too secret and turbulent a lifestyle. Perhaps I was just too much of a dick. I always felt like I had a loyal crew, but when the night was over, the crew was over. There was no continuity, just bright flashes. But boy were those flashes bright.

The city had become my own personal domain. Clubs, bars, and strippers were all part of the weekly agenda. I was still just a teenager, but being nearly six feet tall and broad-shouldered, I rarely caught flak. I left my house every morning and came back the next morning, safe and sound, just a little bit lighter. I lived by the saying, "Early to bed, early to rise, you'll never meet the rich guys."

I normally showed up to the clubs with five to ten thousand dollars in my pockets. It wouldn't be until the next morning that I would realize how much I left with. Sometimes, I would wake up empty. Other times, I would wake up with more than when I had started. Either way, I wouldn't remember what had happened.

Drink tabs would pile up, and VIP entrances were far from cheap. I had to compete with some of the wealthiest men in the city. Walking into such restricted sections was like walking through a Forbes magazine. Everyone was dressed in designer suits, holding thousand-dollar bottles of liquor, throwing money in the air like confetti. I was home. I had no problem substituting a couple days of work for a few hours of being a very important person.

And the girls; don't get me started. They crawled by the tens on their hands and knees just for the opportunity to experience the high life. Everything that their parents had taught them evaporated the minute they saw a little green. I guess I was no different, but at least I wasn't chasing any longer. Once again, I was in the position to sell the illusion of money, to trade body for body, to manipulate people into becoming mine.

Thanks to experiences like these, everything was reduced in my mind. Cars, money, people, even drugs became inconsequential to me, mere toys. I never used drugs dependently, but in the moment, I had no problem committing myself to a new chemical experience. I felt myself to be immortal and always with something to prove. Hardly did the word *no* come out of my mouth.

There came a point when I thought I had already maxed out what life had to offer. I was seventeen, and I had already driven every car, tried every drug, enjoyed every girl, and lived every night. However, this did not dissuade me from carrying on with my lifestyle. In fact, it angered me. I started to force new experiences, not settling for anything that I had already done.

Eventually, I became incapable of doing normal things. School became unbearable. My parents disappeared on my radar. Even work grew boring. I was on a high-speed freeway with no brakes. I either had to run out of gas or crash.

13

There came a day toward the tail end of my senior year when I found myself taking a business test in school. I resented the concept that I, a person already succeeding in business, had to answer to a mere teacher whose entire financial savvy came from a textbook. He always looked to me in class and tried to make me look stupid. He took my frequent absences for weakness without knowing why I was absent in the first place. He compared me to other people in the class, attacked all my errors, and tried to assert his dominance over me. His name was Mr. Ackerly.

Instead of pursuing a relationship with me, Mr. Ackerly only respected the students with the top grades. You know, the students that do all their homework, study hours for each test, jot notes during class, and have their nose shoved far up the teacher's ass. They were the same kids that lived off daddy's high middle-class income and worked summers at Walmart. They all go to college with aspirations of being lawyers or accountants or businessmen or nurses. And they all want to get married, have two kids, and live in a simple suburban home.

Basically, they pride themselves on being boring. But hey, that's what the education system rewards.

On this day in particular, the idea of taking a test made me want to smash my head through the desk. Being here was not only bringing me down, but literally losing me money. And for what cause? To graduate? So that I could spend another four years in school? None of it made sense to me. I was already where I wanted to be and with people that could bring me anywhere I wanted to go.

The test was very difficult. I hadn't been in school for the past week and had no idea what was going on. Usually, I could bullshit my tests by going off acquired business knowledge and common sense. But this material was based on terms that I had never even heard of before. I felt myself failing and, just being who I was, that did not settle well with me. I got angrier with each answer I didn't know. I was a boiling teakettle. When the bell rang, I whistled.

Fuming from the ears, I threw my test on the teacher's desk silently and tried to get through the door as quickly as possible. But Mr. Ackerly stopped me. I heard him yell, "Mr. Ward. Mr. Ward!"

I turned around against the flow of traffic and made my way back into the classroom. Fighting not to explode, I pulled myself back and said, "Yes?"

He knew I was pissed. He wanted to fuck with me. That was the type of guy he was. I hadn't done anything wrong but fail a test. Mr. Ackerly just wanted to kick me while I was down. "Are you okay?"

"Yeah, I'm fine." I itched closer and closer to the door. We were now the only two in the room.

"How was the test?" His voice was so sarcastic, so vile. It was maddening to listen to him talk.

"It was alright."

"All right? Let's go over it together." He was now rummaging through the stack of tests, looking for mine.

Trying to defend myself, I said, "It's really okay. I gotta go to my next class anyway."

Not to be denied, Mr. Ackerly said, "No, no, I'll write you a pass."

He had found my test. He was now sitting down with the answer key and a red pen, marking up my work incessantly. I didn't say anything. I merely took a step back, put my hand on my face, and bowed my head.

Mr. Ackerly finished grading, drew a big "33" on the front of the test, and looked up at me. Obnoxiously, he shrugged and raised his eyebrows. "Thirty-three," he said. "What happened?"

I was pissed. I struck back at him. "Nothing happened. What do you want me to say?"

"Maybe if you would come to class, this wouldn't happen."

"Come to class? Do you have any idea what I do?" Things were getting a bit hostile now.

"No, I don't. Please share."

"Let's just say that what I make in a day"—I pointed at myself—"you make in a month." And I pointed back at him.

"You're such an arrogant little shit." Mr. Ackerly began tensing up his jaw, neck, and fists.

"You wanna see arrogant?" I took off my backpack, unzipped it, and pulled out a stack of five thousand dollars wrapped in a rubber band. I threw it at his chest. "There you go, your month's salary. You're welcome." I put my backpack on and made my way to the door, thinking myself to have won the fight.

His eyes turned red, and I saw all his professionalism collapse. It was now personal. "Yeah, enjoy prison, asshole," I heard from over my shoulder. Mr. Ackerly was not done.

"What did you just say?" I asked, turning around, knowing what he had said, but just wanting him to repeat himself.

"The only place you're going to is prison." His comment didn't even make sense to me. I ignored it altogether.

"Well, it's better than spending every day of my worthless fucking life in a stupid fucking school teaching a bunch of stupid fucking kids!"

"You better watch the way you talk to me, Phineas!" Mr. Ackerly took a step toward me.

"You know what? You're right, Mr. Ackerly." I punched him in the face, knocking him to the floor. I quickly jumped on top, took position, and rained a barrage of punches down on him. He never had the opportunity to strike back. I landed several clean blows, bloodying his lip and nose. It didn't take long until the teachers from the neighboring rooms heard the ruckus and ripped me off him.

Mr. Ackerly was helped up slowly by two other teachers. Still thrilled from the fight, I fought away from the teachers trying to restrain me and said, "Get the fuck off me!" I didn't want anyone touching me. I didn't want anyone looking at me, either, but everyone already was. The room was filled with kids, teachers, security guards, everyone. It was dead quiet.

Eventually, the security guards made their way over to me and said, "C'mon, let's go." I listened, not saying a word. The mob cleared a path for us to walk through, and I made my way to the principal's office. Not a word was shared, not a sound was made. I think the security guards might have been scared themselves.

I was expelled. Mr. Ackerly could've pressed charges but refused to on account that he got his ass beat by a minor. To be honest, I was pretty happy. I was able to kick the shit out of my worst enemy and get away clean. And I didn't have to go to school ever again. I couldn't wait to tell Swezey.

14

There was one consequence that I couldn't avoid. One way or another, I had to go home. And something as bad as this could have definitely awoken the sleeping dragon in my household. My mother and father had accepted silence for about three years, storing up ammunition to strike back one day. That was the day.

I drove home later that night. Five thousand dollars short, I put all my money under the deck and approached the back door. It was locked, so I slowly turned the key trying not to make a sound. I opened the door and sneaked toward the stairs. Both my parents were lounged across the couch, unnoticing. I made it upstairs as slowly as I could. I couldn't believe I was in the clear. Perhaps they really weren't my parents anymore.

It had been a long day and I just wanted to sleep and forget it. I shut the lights off and threw myself onto the bed. I passed out effortlessly.

I was asleep for about twenty minutes until my dream capsized and sank to the bottom of the ocean. Curses began flying around the room. I was being punched all around. Being wrapped in blankets, I couldn't fight back, let alone defend myself. It was dark, and all I could see was shadows. The assailing shadow was broad, tall, and hunched. It had long hair and an amount of fury in every strike. It was my father. I was in a great deal of pain, but all I could do was cringe and squirm away little by little.

I heard my mother screaming from down the hall, "Stop! Stop!" She ran at my dad and tried to pull him off me. She fell to the ground, and my father immediately stopped himself to help her up.

Eventually, the lights flicked on and the beating ceased. My mother was upright again, and my father took a step back to fall in line with her. My mother was distraught and my father was even angrier than he was before. My mother started.

"Why, Phineas? Why are you like this?" Tears were already dripping down her cheeks by the time she had finished speaking.

"Stop calling me Phineas and get the fuck out of my room!" I yelled. I was on a new level of livid. This was the second time today that an adult had gone out of his way to reproach me. At least we had already gotten the fight out of the way.

My father shot back more loudly than I did. "Don't talk to your mother like that!" Once again, someone was telling me how to talk.

In a perfect crescendo, I raised the volume and immediately yelled back at my father. "Fuck you too!" My dad took a hard step forward, but my mother stuck her arm out to restrain him.

"What have we ever done to you?" my mother said. She was now tearfully trembling. The sight of her husband beating her son was too much for her to bear. Her spirit had been damaged, and it showed in every crack of her delicate voice. While she spoke, her body shook and her lower lip shivered.

"Nothing," I said. "You've done nothing. Just get out." I was a revolver on a hot stove top, too hot to move, but too dangerous to let sit.

"No," my mother said. "What did we do wrong?" I could tell that this question had been eating at her mind for some time now.

"I don't know, Mom. Sorry for not being the perfect son." I would have said anything to avoid this conversation. I nearly contemplated jumping out the second-story window.

"We never asked for a perfect son," my mother went on, breaking more with each word.

I immediately fired back in sarcasm, "Well, you didn't get one." They didn't even acknowledge my comment. It was insolence for the sake of insolence and nothing else.

"We just want our son," my mother said, weeping extra loudly at this point. "We gave you everything we could. I don't know what to do anymore." She was so sincere in the sentiments that she expressed. She had poked a hole in my otherwise resolute exterior and now, being exposed and vulnerable, I felt danger. In response, I got angry. My rage forbade me from even opening my mouth to respond. I knew that if the floodgates opened, the devastation would be catastrophic.

My mother looked at me emptily, begging for just a word, a single mumble, anything. Time crawled by slowly.

My mother had faith that I would have the decency to respond, but I was barren, void of all humanity.

"Phineas, say something, please." She prayed for mercy and I handed her shit. Once again, I sat there silently, boiling on the inside about to burst.

And then in the most crushing voice I have ever heard, my mother said, "I'm done. You've broken my heart." She then looked at me one last time, her eyes welling up in tears, and walked out of my room with her head buried in her hands. She was truly broken. Never again would a genuine smile grace her lips. Never again would she be able to live freely without the underlying thoughts of grief and tragedy.

At the moment, I didn't realize the consequences of my action. In fact, I saw myself as the victim. The moment my mother cleared the doorway, I mumbled, "Bye." I was chastising the dead. Not only could I not answer her, but I couldn't even recognize her final farewell. I was a stupid, stupid, stupid kid, and I will never forget that moment.

Before my father followed, he turned to me and said, "I hope you're happy." He held a stare for a brief moment and made his way out. As soon as he was gone, I jolted toward the door, slammed it, and mumbled furiously, "No, I'm done."

I then began to frantically pack as much as I could into a suitcase. Not caring for neatness in my irrational fury, I destroyed the room. Clothes were everywhere. The nightstand had fallen over. My room was in shambles, symbolic of my childhood and home life. Once content, I hustled downstairs with my full suitcase and empty backpack. I grabbed my keys and ran to the back-yard to collect all my money. I filled the bag, jumped in the car, and drove off. I still have yet to return to that house.

It was a dark, misty night. The clouds hid all the stars and the moon hardly peered out. I was alone on the road, in the world, in my mind. I had only one place to go. I was lucky that I even got there.

That night, my car reached upward of 175 MPH. I felt my engine pull and my tires hold on for dear life. I heard the axles squeal and the breaks rip into the wet pavement. The slightest pothole or technical malfunction would have resulted in my utter incineration. I was never even scared. I almost welcomed the end, giving myself up to the laws of nature, science, and religion.

What was normally a thirty-five-minute drive took ten minutes. My car seemed to pant and wheeze once I shut it off at Swezey's mansion. My car knew how lucky it was, but I didn't.

I exited the car, grabbed my baggage, and made my way to the front door. I rang the doorbell and Swezey answered. Not saying a word, he looked me in the eyes, nodded solemnly, and gestured me to come inside.

15

Waking up the next morning, I felt an unexpected sense of serenity. I woke up in an elegant, king-size bed with a white, tufted headboard and a silky, gray comforter. The room was spacious on every side of the bed. The marble tile floor made it seem as if the low-lying bed was sliding on ice. Both my suitcase and backpack rested on top of a glossy, white dresser against the wall to my left. Light permeated through the wall of windows to my right and reflected off every inch of the room, filling the space with radiance and energy. I merely sat upright, still wrapped in the covers, admiring the scene and silence.

On that day, I was perfectly happy with just existing. I didn't want to work or talk or leave the house. I wanted to wander around freely and let my mind tag along. Everything was bright and simple. All my worries were miles away, and I had no desire to chase them.

When I came down the stairs, I was overjoyed to see Swezey making breakfast. He looked at me, smiled, and said, "There he is. How you feeling, big guy?" Swezey was always happy to see me.

I sat down on a high wooden stool at a marble island. I laid my head down on my arms so that I could still face Swezey at the stove. "Great," I said. "Great."

Swezey looked back at me, almost surprised. "Good to hear," Swezey remarked. He didn't believe me, but he let it be. Swezey always minded his own business. He cared, but he knew his limits and understood that it was sometimes best to give space. He never even asked me about what had happened that night. He knew I needed him and that was it. It didn't matter what for or how long. That was the type of relationship we had.

"What are we doing today?" I asked Swezey.

"You tell me. I took off work."

"Why?"

"Why? Because I own the damn company and I can do whatever I want." He looked at me and smiled.

"Let's go to the beach."

"Alright, eat, get ready, and we'll leave in thirty minutes." He slid a plate of eggs toward me and disappeared into another room. Swezey always seemed to make the slickest entrances and exits. He always seemed to say the right thing and make the right move.

Despite the fact that Swezey lived on a beach himself, we drove for two hours to the nicest beach in the state. We took his favorite car, a two-seater convertible worth over half a million dollars. Over the course of the ride, we did not exchange one word or listen to one second of the radio. Instead, we relished in the encompassing, cloudless blue sky, the passing mounds of sand and plants, the crisp, cool wind drumming our faces.

The sun spotlighted us the entire trip, ensuring us that we were never alone, never without help. The road was always in front of us, never underneath or behind.

Swezey was the man I aspired to one day become, a model to replicate, the father I always wanted. We were comfortable together. There was never the pressure to fill in silence with empty and meaningless chatter. It was enough to bask in each other's presence and simply exist as one. It was an understood, unspoken agreement between the two of us.

We sat on the beach next to each other, arms behind us supporting our weight, looking out into the crashing and curling of the ocean. Swezey finally broke the silence and said, "You turn eighteen in a couple weeks, right?"

"Ten days," I replied.

"You know what that means, right?"

It could have meant a whole host of things, but I didn't know specifically what answer he was looking for. "I don't know. I can go to the doctor by myself?" I joked.

Swezey shook his head and grinned. "You really don't remember? You don't remember busting my balls when you were a little fourteen-year-old?"

I felt bad. I tried to remember back to my summer training, but so much had happened from then to now that I couldn't remember too many singular events. I only retained the teachings that I had applied every day since. "No."

"When you were fourteen, you asked me if you could invest, remember?" His face got serious but mine lit up.

"Oh, yeah."

"And I told you when you turned eighteen, we'd do it."

I became very excited. I didn't care what it entailed. I just needed a change of pace. "Awesome. Let's do it."

"I already have something good lined up, but I'm not gonna get into it right now. Let's just enjoy the day."

And we did. I nodded and respected his desire to put off the topic for later. It was not easy, but I managed. I just shut my mind back off and let myself drift in the breeze, into the graceful tide of the ocean.

16

The next morning, Swezey sat down with me at the dinner table to discuss the investment. This time, there were no eggs, just black coffee. We were speaking business, and he didn't want me mistaking that.

Swezey did not reveal much about the ins and outs of the investment. In fact, he did not say much about anything. All he disclosed was that the project aimed to reach out and assist struggling businesses for a tail-end profit. He painted a cloudy picture that I did not wholly understand, but believed in nonetheless.

Bottom line, he didn't have to sell me anything. Four years of anticipation coupled with my respect and trust for Swezey made skepticism implausible. I knew he wouldn't let me down, especially in my first foray into the investing world. Swezey was opening a new door for me, and I was not about to turn around and lock myself in my room.

The base investment that Swezey proposed was $250,000 from both me and him. That way, we could hold substantial ownership in the project and strategically use such power to further our income. Swezey would handle all the finer points. All I needed to do was dip my toe in and sit back.

$250,000 is a significant amount of money for anybody, not to mention a seventeen-year-old. I had the money, but it would be painful to hand over. However, I wasn't about to look small. I made sure not to hesitate or express any doubt in my acceptance. I was all in, making my way to the next level.

After our talk, I ran upstairs and checked all the money in my bag. I counted fifty-two stacks of five thousand, a total of $260,000. I counted it three times in disbelief. Where had all the money gone? I first hypothesized that I had been robbed, but eventually realized the cruel truth of it all.

I had never noticed the curse of my spending habits until that moment. Once a seventeen-year-old millionaire, I was a couple minutes from having only ten grand to my name. I was back to where I had started when I first met Swezey at the age of fourteen. It was the same stack of money he had given me after throwing my backpack out his window. I felt empty, without purpose, stuck on a treadmill working toward nowhere.

Swezey had no clue how dire my financial situation was at the time. He knew I was never much of a miser, but not to this extent. He had often encouraged me to save, but I had neglected to do so. In my mind, I couldn't tell him. I had to bite my tongue, carry through with the investment, and hope for light on the other side. In the meantime, I would just have to survive.

I put $250,000 in my backpack and stuffed the rest underneath the hollow bottom of the dresser. I walked downstairs with the backpack to where Swezey was still sitting and reading the newspaper. I approached him and plopped the bag down on the table. He looked at me, smirked keenly, raised his coffee mug up, and winked. He never opened the backpack.

I didn't say or do anything. I felt guilty withholding my dilemma from him and foolish giving the last of my money away. Thinking of it today, I should've been direct and honest. He would not have been angry with me, perhaps disappointed, but I had too much pride to say no, too much to prove to myself.

After giving Swezey the money, I walked into the backyard and sat on a lounge chair overlooking the pool. I looked up at the gray, murky sky and down on the correspondingly dull water. The trees did not sway or shine. Birds were not singing and bees were not buzzing. There was not even a breeze to keep me company. Surrounded by nature, I saw no life. I felt lifeless myself.

Looking into the small plot of forestry at the farthest end of the property, I saw bushes shake and shadows jump. I heard a rustling. Some form of life was with me in this colorless, empty world. I sat up in my chair to observe. There was hope.

The suspense built with each passing moment until a deer hopped out of the trees. It was beautiful. Its lavish, light brown coat triumphed over its dull background. Its light feet and jovial demeanor brightened the vibe of each space it filled. Prancing around, the deer spanned the width of the yard but never came within twenty feet of me.

Suddenly, the deer stopped and spotted me. It was as surprised as I was when I saw it. Motionless, we maintained eye contact for about five seconds. The deer then quickly turned and sprinted back into the trees.

It was once again the same dark world, but now I knew that beauty was out there somewhere. It would come again one day. I would just have to wait.

17

That next week, I turned the page on a prior way of living. I worked and worked and worked and didn't spend a dime. Instead of visiting ten houses a day, I found my way to fifteen. And instead of selling three or four investments, I sold five or six. I was tenacious, refusing to take no for an answer, driven by desperation and failure. I made over forty thousand dollars in seven days.

The panic of being broke had jump-started the fervor that thrived in me as a child. I was no longer working for the nightlife or the girls or the toys. It was all about those lovely little greenbacks again. I sought refuge in money. It stabilized and comforted me. It pushed me to ignore unhealthy temptation. It helped me move on.

At the end of the span, I was exhausted but not weak. In fact, I was stronger than ever. But more importantly, I had made Swezey proud. It was through him that I had found the strength to change. It was through myself that I would find the strength to keep going.

Driving home from work at the end of the week, I found Swezey's street to be particularly quiet and dark. There were many cars parked on the street, but not a person in sight. As I made my way farther down the street, I began to hear an echo. The ground even seemed to start shaking. Swezey's mansion was concealed by a long curve in the road. It was all the way at the end of the court.

I itched closer and closer to the bend, greatly anticipating what would reveal itself on the other side. The sound grew with each roll. Before long, I saw it. The lights, the music, the people. It was unbelievable. I covered my mouth in amazement and laughed all the way into the driveway.

Swezey's mansion was lit up like the sky on the Fourth of July. Herds of people poured into the house and backyard. Music reverberated throughout the entire block. It was a party at Swezey's and everybody was invited.

When I walked through the door, I was greeted by a zoo. Hundreds of people were scattered about the house, dressed in wily colors and invigorated by copious amounts of alcohol. Despite the overwhelming lack of space, the partygoers were not remaining still. They were flying across the room in gleeful play.

At the party, there were people of all ages and backgrounds. The large majority of people were adults, perhaps friends or business associates of Swezey's. There were some kids, but few I had ever seen before. Many young adults that supposedly lived in the area had made their way to the house as well. There were caterers dressed in tuxedos, serving drinks and food to everyone. And upstairs, there were ten strippers.

Some would ask how a party like this could survive into the night. But those people weren't at the party and wouldn't know that the entire local police force was in attendance. They were amid all normal civilians, engorging themselves with no exception. Some were even in uniform with their patrol cars parked outside.

In the far back right corner of the house was a bar. Behind the bar was a beautifully stacked pyramid of assorted liquor bottles. People would take whole bottles for themselves, and the pyramid would just regenerate as if nothing had happened. The supply was bottomless, and people rejoiced accordingly.

Outside, a whole new world appeared. The lives of the rich and famous had all converged on this night. Supermodels adorned the pool. Celebrities sat at tables together. Prominent social figures shared discussions on the outskirts of the party. It was the VIP section, except instead of one room, it was a five-acre backyard.

I wandered in astonishment. I hadn't even taken my backpack off or changed out of my work clothes. I was mystified, entrapped in the impossibilities that surrounded me. All my wildest fantasies had come to fruition, and I couldn't do anything but wonder how. I felt like I was in outer space, floating weightlessly among the unknown, bearing witness to phenomena most people only dream of.

Eventually, I was alone. I had walked far enough that I had no one on either side of me. I now looked back on it all. The chaos had not ceased in the slightest. All along eye level, I could not see a speck of idleness, silence, or depth. But as my eyes itched up farther and farther, I began to see a contrast. Light and dark, life and death, it all showed among the architecture of the house.

Perched on the second-floor balcony of the house was a DJ, the heart of the party, pumping blood to each little vein below. Above him was an even higher balcony connected to the master bedroom. There, darkness appeared to settle without a disturbance. It seemed empty. But if you were to look closely or even with a pair of sober eyes, you would see a shadow.

Standing atop his mountain, overseeing all he had created, was the brain of the party. He stood calmly with his arms crossed, pacing back and forth across the balcony. I could only see the shape of his figure and how the night sky wrapped around him. He shared the party with the stars, blessing their beauty with his company. It was Swezey.

I immediately sought to join him. I made my way through the backyard, the house, and up the stairs. This lap through was not nearly as sensational as the first. I was numb to it now, frozen to a new focus. Before long, I was past it all. It was just a house again.

I walked through Swezey's bedroom to the third-floor balcony. I saw Swezey from behind. An unopened cut glass bottle of scotch lay at his feet. He was motionless.

I walked up and leaned on the railing next to him. He didn't turn to me or say anything. We just took in the moment together.

I looked down at the party below. The scene embodied the beautiful disorder of humanity. The lights flashing upon the beautiful landscape in the night humbled Swezey and me. I felt as if I were trapped in a combination painting by Van Gogh, Rembrandt, and Pollock. My eyes were shocked, but my ears remained unscathed. From my perspective, all was silent. The sight spoke for itself.

"Some night, huh?" Swezey broke the silence. His voice was unlike anything I had ever heard before. It was soft and exasperated, the voice of a man fresh off a night of thought.

"It's amazing," I responded, still in awe.

Silence then permeated back into the night, as the conversation temporarily stopped.

"You know, Feeney," Swezey interjected once again, "I'm very proud of you."

I changed my focus to Swezey, now turning my head to face him. He continued to look out.

"You've already done so much at such a young age," Swezey continued. "You're gonna do great things one day."

"Thanks," I said, choked up with emotion.

"Don't thank me. You've done it all yourself." Swezey then lifted the bottle of scotch off the ground along with two glasses. He poured them and handed one to me. We clinked glasses and each took a sip. We were back where we had started four years ago.

"How would it sound if I gave you that pool house?" Swezey asked out of nowhere. "You could stay in there, have your own place."

"That'd be great," I said.

"Well, it's yours then." I fought to stay cool. "You can move in there tomorrow morning."

"Thanks." I was so happy. "What time are we going into work tomorrow?"

"Forget about work! You worked your ass off this week. Enjoy yourself. Take two weeks off." I needed to work. I had a lot of money to make up, and two weeks without pay wouldn't help matters.

"But—"

"But nothing. Relax, I'll give you some cash to spend if you really need it."

"Why—why are you doing all this?" I was now very confused. I didn't know what was going on. Swezey had always been very generous and kind with me, but this was almost excessive.

"What are you talking about?" Swezey finished his glass, stood up straight, and walked toward the door to his room. "I'm going to bed, Feeney." He stood in the doorway, empty glass in his hand, looking at me.

"Alright, Swezey, good night," I said, a little annoyed that I couldn't get an actual answer.

Swezey nodded and disappeared into the darkness of his room. I turned back to the view of the party. It was still in full force, but duller in my mind. I was tired, but I knew I wouldn't be able to sleep. My thoughts were far too active.

From behind me, I heard Swezey's voice. "And, Feeney." He paused. "Happy birthday." Swezey disappeared again, and I was left alone, stunned and speechless.

It was my eighteenth birthday.

18

The party had lasted well into the night, far past the departure of the host. For some, the party had never ended. They woke the next morning in the same house they had spent the night in, disheveled and confused, void of memory and shame. One by one, they gathered their things and left the property. Neither Swezey nor I had said anything to them.

Once the rest of the stragglers made their way off the floor and out the door, I sat down on the couch in utter exhaustion. I hadn't gotten drunk or even participated in the festivities, but I still hadn't slept much. The party had kept me up most of the night, leaving me in bed with my eyes open.

I lulled in and out of consciousness on Swezey's black, modern sofa. I sank into a cloud of my own lucid dreams, wondering what was real and what wasn't. Everything was foreign and unbelievable to the eye. But my memory from the night before promised me that I was not seeing a mirage or a vision or a large collection of shadows. The evidence was all there. Swezey had thrown the greatest party of all time just for me, and I had barely shown up.

The only thing to pull me out of my semiconscious meditation was the doorbell. To my dismay, I feebly lifted myself off the couch and dragged myself to the door. I opened it to the sight of a dozen maids in a well-ordered, double-filed formation. They entered the house without saying a word and immediately got to work. Not wasting a second to breathe, they turned the house right side up. I didn't think much of it. I just collapsed back on the couch and closed my eyes.

Early into my dozing, I felt the light breathing of another and then an even lighter tap on my shoulder. I opened my eyes to see one of the cleaning ladies hovering over me. I was a bit startled but too tired to react.

"Excuse me, sir," she said. "I think there is a letter for you." She had a strong Hispanic accent, but a delicate tone. She gestured over to the kitchen counter.

Not saying anything, I rose up from the couch and walked to the kitchen. The letter was from Swezey. It read:

Feeney,

I had to run out early. I'll be back tomorrow morning.

Swezey

I hadn't even noticed that Swezey was gone. But the letter reminded me of our conversation from the previous night. I had two weeks off, and the pool house was mine to live in. In excitement, I immediately darted up the stairs to pack all my things.

When I reached my bedroom, I was horrified. All my stuff was gone. My closet and dresser were empty. Everything was cleared out of my bathroom. Worst of all, my backpack was nowhere to be found. Forty thousand dollars, vanished without a trace.

I checked in my stowaway spot underneath the dresser and found my original ten thousand dollars. Normally, I would've hidden the money the minute I got home, but the party had knocked me off track. I was still the same stupid kid.

I put the ten thousand dollars in my pocket and walked angrily to the pool house to find a new hiding spot. Each step infuriated me more and more. The rage within me grew and twisted into a tornado of fiery regret and self-deprecation. I was so fucking stupid! I couldn't believe I didn't protect the one thing that had kept my life stable.

When I opened the door to the pool house, I was shocked. Swezey had not only moved all my belongings into the house, but he set up gifts wishing me a happy eighteenth birthday. A banner overlooked the entrance. A bottle of fine scotch with a red bow sat on the coffee table. A small pile of wrapped boxes rested in the corner of the living room.

All my things were in the bedroom. The clothes, shoes, and money were accounted for, along with some new items with fresh tags on them. Swezey had taken me in as his own and given me a new life.

For the record, this pool house was far from the average supply shack. More than anything else, it resembled a high-class condo you would find actors living in during the summer. It had a bathroom, a kitchen, a living space, and a bedroom. The interior was finely furnished with modern wooden adornments and complex decorations. A beautiful entertainment center pillared the house. The crystal and stainless steel center was flush with foreign relics and glassware, and a huge flat-screen television hung above it all. The house made the most of its volume, but was in no way cramped or uncomfortable. It was a great area to kick back and relax, to be alone. It was simple, yet perfect.

For the remainder of the day, I sat in my new home and did nothing. It was beautiful. All alone cloaked in pure serenity, I felt myself drift. For the first time in a while, I was content with idleness, satisfied with stagnancy. Moving would only be detrimental. I was happy where I was.

However, at night, I began to wonder. Where had my $250,000 truly gone? I had questions that Swezey hadn't entertained. I was in no way spiteful; I just had nothing to do but consider the thoughts that were sticking to my mind. In an attempt to uncover some further information, I left the pool house and entered the main mansion.

I began probing through Swezey's office. I felt bad violating his privacy with no grounds for suspicion. This man had done nothing but pamper me, and I had the audacity to question his word. I was being nosy for no reason other than boredom. I knew it was wrong, but was nonetheless interested in the other side that Swezey had kept from me for the past four years.

I rummaged through his filing cabinets, his desks, his drawers, even his loose papers. I saw nothing that even slightly jogged my memory. None of his clients seemed to match mine.

Eventually, I had made it through everything. All that remained for me to search was the closet. Already coming this far, I didn't hesitate. I threw the door open and started thumbing through his coats and then the shelf above them. On the floor of the closet, I saw four cardboard boxes the sizes of nightstands, jutting out.

Each box was designated with a marking. They were labeled: *1, 2, 3, 4.* Each one also had my name written on it: *Feeney.* Suspicious, I moved all the coats aside and pulled out box #1. It had substantial weight to it.

I opened the box and examined what was inside. There were many stuffed envelopes and one marble notebook. The envelopes were each assigned a number and filled with thousands of dollars in cash. The notebook detailed the money using a chart consisting of five columns: *Number, Name, Principal, Commission, Net.* I recognized all the names. They were my first clients.

In disbelief, I counted all the money in every envelope. Each matched an entry in the notebook with 10% of the principal missing. I began to recollect all the sales as they had happened four years prior.

I approached the closet again and tried to pull out the second box. It would hardly even budge. The box had to weigh at least two hundred pounds. After a great deal of tugging, the box ripped and fell over on its side. Cash poured out. The insides corresponded with the first one, just in a larger proportion. The notebook precisely reflected my second year of sales.

The next two boxes were physically immovable. Each housing around ten million dollars, the boxes far outweighed me. It was still the same story. Coincidence had gone out the window.

I was horrified, dismayed, destroyed. I sought for something, anything to prove my thoughts wrong. I meticulously checked everything once and twice and three times. Before long, I lost hope.

All the money I had handed over the past four years went no farther than Swezey's hand. All I had learned, all I had worked for was nothing but accomplice to theft. He took advantage of my childish innocence for his own selfish gain. And to think I saw him as a role model, a father.

I felt my mind explode. I was a volcano of pain, torching all in my path and inevitably destroying myself. How could I have been blinded for so long? I was his personal assassin, his puppet. He pulled all my strings and turned me into an act, a show designed to rip into poor innocent people and their wallets.

Throbbing in fury, I thought back to why I was in Swezey's office in the first place. I was as much a victim as anyone else. I had just given him $250,000! *Investments?!* I was just another ATM for him and nothing more. Our entire relationship was a scam, a hoax. I was more alone than ever, and in my solitude, I would change. Never again would I be toyed with.

Broken and bursting at the seams, I grabbed a hand truck from the garage and transported each box, one by one, to the pool house. It took four trips to move about twenty-five million dollars. Everything I had once known and committed myself to was up in flames. Now, all I could do was stand by, stricken in horror, a mere spectator to the blaze.

19

After I had set all the boxes down, I collapsed on the floor. I was overcome and paralyzed with feelings, emotions I couldn't even begin to understand. Angry, confused, distraught, lost, alone, betrayed, embarrassed, depressed. Tears flowed from my eyes without a hope of stopping.

Fearful of my vulnerability, I felt a rush of adrenaline course through my veins and yank me off the floor. I was now wired, and as a result, all my passive emotions seemed to subside. The only one that remained was anger. And it took over.

I paced restlessly. I began uncontrollably snarling and grimacing to myself. I was entering a dark, dark place. With each step, the way out got farther away. It eventually disappeared, leaving me alone.

Eventually, emotions weren't enough for me. I needed to take action. That was the only way I could bring justice to myself and the other victims. Something had to be done to this deceitful, conniving man. But what, I did not know.

I thought of turning him into the police. But then, I thought about the team of lawyers that Swezey would assemble. And where would a criminal investigation leave me? God forbid Swezey did get convicted, I would be left unemployed, broke, and homeless. Or even worse, he could pull me down with him. There was no way for that option to benefit me. It would be a personal sacrifice for the solace of strangers.

Maybe I would just confront him, man to man. I would demand that he came clean, and he would laugh in my face. He had all the leverage, the money, and the respect. The truth didn't mean anything when I had no means of exposing it. He could make me disappear whenever he wanted.

I could've killed him. I could have. Lord knows that at the time, I would have. If he were home, he probably would have been sitting in his leather armchair, watching the news, dozing in and out of consciousness. He might have been drunk, glass in hand or on the small table to his right. I could have silently grabbed a knife from the kitchen and made my way behind him. He would never have detected me if I were careful. Coming from the back door, my path would have never crossed his line of vision.

Standing behind him, I would have held the knife against his throat. I might have shared some sentiment with him first, maybe explaining my actions or forcing him to explain his. Or maybe, I just would have sliced, leaving him to die without a reason, without time to say good-bye. And like that, he would be dead. Justice would be served.

I felt evil showering over me. Never before had I contemplated killing another, especially not my childhood idol. Tides had turned so abruptly that I had no opportunity to approach the situation rationally. Only primal instincts were quick enough to react. I fell to savagery as a result.

I looked around the room frantically. I saw the unopened presents. In anger, I bolted toward them and crushed them underneath my feet. I then recklessly swung kicks, sending the gifts flying across the room. I drove my fist into the sixty-inch television hanging against the wall and continued to swat everything in sight. The television fell and shattered through the entertainment center. Before long, the room was empty and the floor was carpeted with the remains. Anything that seemed breakable was broken, except for one thing.

The cut glass bottle of scotch called to me from the coffee table. It sang to me. It promised that it would heal all my fresh wounds, soothe my weeping heart. I began to drink directly out of the bottle. I guzzled until I physically couldn't any longer. I was drunk before the bottle left my lips. It didn't stop the pain. It just made action easier.

I stumbled over to the boxes and looked down at all the loose stacks of money and empty envelopes. All this money had at one point passed through my fingers in check form. Was I going to let it escape from my grasp once more? I couldn't do that twice in a lifetime. I hustled to the kitchen and grabbed a box of matches.

On the way back, I snatched the bottle of scotch, took a swig, grabbed the hand truck, and moved each box onto the back lawn. I emptied the boxes into a glorious mountain of cash and began to douse it in liquor.

Watching the alcohol cascade down the mountainside, I lit a match and proceeded to burn twenty-five million dollars.

I don't remember anything else from that night.

20

I came to the next morning, extremely hungover, alone in my new and ruined pool house. I was sprawled out on the floor, surrounded by broken glass. At the time, I couldn't recall much of what had happened the night before. I rolled over on my stomach and slowly lifted myself up. I then sat on a nearby armchair, trying to put the pieces from the previous night together.

I scanned the room and was dismayed by the destruction. Order had fallen to chaos and now all that remained was the quiet aftermath. It was the cool, eerie morning after a long, bloody battle. The surroundings whispered of the fight. Everything was an enigma, but it would all begin to make sense.

My cell phone rang. It was located on the small table next to the chair I was sitting in. Aside the phone was my black, leather ledger of sales. My book was always in my backpack, so I had no clue how it had gotten there. I thought deeply, but my mind was a blank slate.

The phone call was from a number I didn't recognize, so I didn't answer. After the phone stopped ringing, I briefly checked my notifications and found thirty missed calls from different numbers. I was startled, but being so mentally feeble and fatigued, I didn't bother to stress over it. I shut the phone off and put it in my pocket.

After a few minutes of sitting thoughtlessly, I heard the sound of a car door slam. It was Swezey. With it returned my anger from the night before. But this time, I was more clear and calm in my anger. This time, it was manageable.

I would merely approach him and let him know that our relationship was over. I would then walk out of his life forever. Where I would go, I did not know. But I had to stand up for what was right and accept the consequences as they followed. The past four years of my life were over. I was now my own man.

I calmly walked out of the pool house and toward Swezey's mansion. As I neared closer, the mansion seemed larger. It began to tower over me. The magnificence of the house imposed itself upon me, aiming to intimidate. However, I would not cower. It was my responsibility, my duty to remain strong and bring the giant down. I, the courageous David, was marching before Swezey, the mighty Goliath, armed with my better knowledge and resolution, my loyal slingshot.

Before long, I was at the castle gates. I took a deep breath, knowing that there was no going back once I crossed the other side. I closed my eyes and envisioned all that Swezey had brought to my life. I thought of how he had openly welcomed me off the streets and into his home. I pondered how Swezey had sculpted me into the man I was that day. And then, I considered how he had taken all that our relationship had meant, all that we had been through together and crushed it beneath his feet just to make an extra buck. I was ready.

I opened the door confidently as a merchant of truth. However, the wind was taken out of my sails by the sound of Swezey's voice.

"Good morning, Feeney!" He paused and turned around to look at me. He was standing at the stove with a sinister grin on his face. He was making eggs. "Looks like you had a fun night." Swezey knew hungover when he saw it. "Sit down. I'm making breakfast."

I was speechless. Everything that I had planned to say was now running for cover, scurrying chaotically throughout my mind. I worked to reorganize it, but there was not much hope. Swezey's sweet and harmless demeanor made him impossible to reproach, even when he was in the wrong. The fucker was making me eggs for crying out loud! I was out of my league.

Swezey didn't continue the conversation. He just cooked while I sat at the center island. I eventually settled upon initiating my statement. I figured that once the wheels started rolling, the engine would take over from there. I was nervous. All my conviction had melted away. I didn't know how to begin.

"Swezey," I muttered. It almost sounded like a question. It wasn't an ideal start, but I got his attention. He looked up.

"Yeah?" Swezey wondered. He looked me in the eyes longingly, truly concerned in what I had to say. He even seemed worried for me, as if I were in trouble and needed help. However, before I could get into the real issue, there was a loud knock at the door. There was a slight pause, and then three more knocks. Swezey snapped his head to the door and back. "One second," he said to me and raised his pointer finger.

Swezey walked to the door quickly, not wanting to ignore whatever issue I was about to unveil. He disappeared into the next room. I heard the door open and then a deafening gunshot. The sound echoed throughout the house and around my mind, jolting me out of my seat and toward the door.

At the front door, I saw a tall, burly man carrying a revolver in his right hand. On the ground lay Swezey's cold, lifeless body. There was a bullet in his head. Blood coated the floor. The house was still. There was not a sound or movement.

I looked up to the shooter and made eye contact. My blood immediately froze within my veins. I felt a chill course up through my spine. My jaw dropped and my eyes dilated. I was paralyzed, trapped in my own horror. The man who had shot Swezey was a recent client of mine.

He maintained eye contact with me for a few seconds, turned around, and casually walked away. He never raised his gun to me, never even looked down at the body. I never saw that man again, but he would forever live inside me.

I had called him the night before. I had called all my clients the night before, informing them about Swezey's actions. I was the one who had killed Swezey.

21

Today, I sit atop an empire that I do not deserve. I am a figurehead of no real substance or worth. I was not elected nor appointed. Technicality dropped the sword upon my shoulder, and since then, that sword has continued to dig deeper and deeper.

Almost a year has passed since Swezey's death. Now, I finally have the life I always dreamed of. I was the only name mentioned in Swezey's will. He left me everything. The house, the cars, all the money, everything. I was my five-year-old self's idol, but my current self's nemesis.

There is no longer anything left to chase in my life. Sixty years of retirement wait before me. I can travel the world, buy an island, even fall in love. But inside, I am not worth a breath of fresh air. I deserve to spend the rest of my life in a prison cell. At least there, I could sleep. I could go a night without being haunted by what I have done.

I don't understand how Swezey lived in this house alone for all those years. I can hear my thoughts echo off the walls. Sometimes, I even feel lost, without a next move and without a purpose.

Unlike Swezey, I do not have the luxury of an escape. Swezey Co. is in ruins, and I lay buried underneath. The weight keeps me down, while the debris horrifies me with what was. I am an artifact, a mere remnant of the past. Modern times have no use for me. And as a result, I lay fruitlessly, collecting dust and mourning my loss.

Many months ago when the will was being read, I found a letter hidden in Swezey's desk. It was addressed for my eyes only. Every day, I have looked at that envelope, fearful of what was inside. But now, I know the pain cannot grow any worse. It is time to face yet another challenge. It is time to hear his voice one last time.

Feeney,

I apologize for not telling you earlier, but I have left. And I will not return. I plan on spending the rest of my life away, bouncing around from country to country, living simply. Do not miss me, for you must know that I will be in a better place. You must also know that I was not a happy man.

For years, I have partaken in practices that have ruined the lives of others. At first, the money thrilled me, but now, it is the root of my suffering. Even more painful is the thought that I dragged you into it. I am very sorry, Feeney. I have betrayed you. All the money that you have brought in over the years will be used to fund the rest of my days. Although I have my regrets, I thank you. Without you, I would not have the strength to move on. I would not have known that there was something left to chase.

As for our $500,000 investment, I gave it to your parents as a present from you. It will revive their business *and allow you to reconnect with them. Do not reject them for the living they make or the life they live or how much they love you. They are wonderful people and deserve you more than I. I urge you from the bottom of my heart to show your parents what you've shown me over the past four years.*

As for everything else, it is yours. It's always been yours. Use it to start over, to build something of your own. I am nothing to replicate. Like I said before, you will do great things one day. You have everything you need. Don't let greed possess you. Create, don't manipulate. Work for a greater cause. These are the simple things in life that I avoided, but long for today.

You have brought more joy to my life than any amount of money ever could. You are my greatest investment. I will miss you dearly, but anxiously await watching you grow into your own man.

So carry on. Find a love for life and never let it go. There will be moments when the road will split and time will press on you to make a sacrifice. Never let that sacrifice be yourself. Forever live in the mind of a young entrepreneur.

Swezey

Made in the USA
Lexington, KY
11 February 2015